GW00501801

A Christmas Miscellany

Money donated to Traidcraft Exchange from the sale of this book could help small-scale farmers and producers in the developing world gain the confidence, knowledge and skills they need to trade their way out of poverty.

To find out more about how you can help Traidcraft create a world free from the scandal of poverty where all people and their communities can flourish, visit: www.traidcraft.org.uk

Traidcraft Exchange - registered charity number 1048752

TRAIDCRAFT
Fighting poverty through trade

A Christmas Miscellany

Edited by Simon Danes

TRADECRAFT
Fighting poverty through trade

ST MARK'S PRESS

Published by St Mark's Press, 20 Close Road, Pavenham, MK43 7PP, UK

If Jesus was born today
copyright © Steve Turner 2012

All other original material copyright © Simon Danes 2012

Illustrations by Alison Hullyer copyright © Alison Hullyer 2012. Visit www.hullyer.co.uk

Cover design by Tony Cantale Graphics
and Full Stop Design

All rights reserved. No part of this publication may be reproduced, stored in a retrieval system, or transmitted, in any form or by any means, electronic, mechanical, photocopying, recording or otherwise, without prior permission.

The moral rights of the authors have been asserted.

Printed and bound in the UK by Henry Ling Ltd., Dorchester.

www.stmarkspress.com

CONTENTS

Fiction and Prose

Poetry

All the trimmings

Fiction and Prose

Sherlock Holmes *in*

The Adventure of the Blue Carbuncle

Arthur Conan Doyle

I had called upon my friend Sherlock Holmes upon the second morning after Christmas, with the intention of wishing him the compliments of the season. He was lounging upon the sofa in a purple dressing-gown, a pipe-rack within his reach upon the right, and a pile of crumpled morning papers, evidently newly studied, near at hand. Beside the couch was a wooden chair, and on the angle of the back hung a very seedy and disreputable hard-felt hat, much the worse for wear, and cracked in several places. A lens and a forceps lying upon the seat of the chair suggested that the hat had been suspended in this manner for the purpose of examination.

'You are engaged,' said I; 'perhaps I interrupt you.'

'Not at all. I am glad to have a friend with whom I can discuss my results. The matter is a perfectly trivial one' – he jerked his thumb in the direction of the old hat – 'but there are points in connection with it which are not entirely devoid of interest and even of instruction.'

I seated myself in his armchair and warmed my hands before his crackling fire, for a sharp frost had set in, and the windows were thick with the ice crystals. 'I suppose,' I remarked, 'that, homely as it looks, this thing has some deadly story linked on to it – that it is the clue which will guide you in the solution of some mystery and the punishment of some crime.'

'No, no. No crime,' said Sherlock Holmes, laughing. 'Only one of those whimsical little incidents which will happen when you have four million human beings all jostling each other within the space of a few square miles. Amid the action and reaction of so dense a swarm of humanity, every possible combination of events may be expected to take place, and many a little problem will be presented which may be striking and bizarre without being criminal. We have already had experience of such.'

'So much so,' I remarked, 'that of the last six cases which I have added to my notes, three have been entirely free of any legal crime.'

'Precisely. You allude to my attempt to recover the Irene Adler papers, to the singular case of Miss Mary Sutherland, and to the adventure of the man with the twisted lip. Well, I have no doubt that this small matter will fall into the same innocent category. You know Peterson, the commissionaire?'

'Yes.'

'It is to him that this trophy belongs.'

'It is his hat.'

'No, no, he found it. Its owner is unknown. I beg that you will look upon it not as a battered billycock but as an intellectual problem. And, first, as to how it came here. It arrived upon Christmas morning, in company with a good fat goose, which is, I have no doubt, roasting at this moment in front of Peterson's fire. The facts are these: about four o'clock on Christmas morning, Peterson, who, as you know, is a very honest fellow, was returning from some small jollification and was making his way homeward down Tottenham Court Road. In front of him he saw, in the gaslight, a tallish man, walking with a slight stagger, and carrying a white goose slung over his shoulder. As he reached the corner of Goodge Street, a row broke out between this stranger and a little knot of roughs. One of the latter knocked off the man's hat, on which he raised his stick to defend himself and, swinging it over his head, smashed the shop window behind him. Peterson had rushed forward to protect the stranger from his assailants; but the man, shocked at having broken the window, and seeing an official-looking person in uniform rushing towards him, dropped his goose, took to his heels, and vanished amid the labyrinth of small streets which lie at the back of Tottenham Court Road. The roughs had also fled at the appearance of Peterson, so that he was left in possession of the field of battle, and also of the spoils of victory in the shape of this battered hat and a most unimpeachable Christmas goose.'

'Which surely he restored to their owner?'

'My dear fellow, there lies the problem. It is true that "For Mrs Henry Baker" was printed upon a small card which was tied to the bird's left leg, and it is also true that the initials "H. B." are legible upon the lining of this hat, but as there are some thousands of Bakers, and some hundreds of Henry Bakers in this city of ours, it is not easy to restore lost property to any one of them.'

'What, then, did Peterson do?'

'He brought round both hat and goose to me on Christmas morning, knowing that even the smallest problems are of interest to me. The goose we retained until this morning, when there were signs that, in spite of the slight frost, it would be well that it should be eaten without unnecessary delay. Its finder has carried it off, therefore, to fulfill the ultimate destiny of a goose, while I continue to retain the hat of the unknown gentleman who lost his Christmas dinner.'

'Did he not advertise?'

'No.'

'Then, what clue could you have as to his identity?'

'Only as much as we can deduce.'

'From his hat?'

'Precisely.'

'But you are joking. What can you gather from this old battered felt?'

'Here is my lens. You know my methods. What can you gather yourself as to the individuality of the man who has worn this article?'

I took the tattered object in my hands and turned it over rather ruefully. It was a very ordinary black hat of the usual round shape, hard and much the worse for wear. The lining had been of red silk, but was a good deal discoloured. There was no maker's name; but, as Holmes had remarked, the initials "H. B." were scrawled upon one side. It was pierced in the brim for a hat-securer, but the elastic was missing. For the rest, it was cracked, exceedingly dusty, and spotted in several places, although there seemed to have been some attempt to hide the discoloured patches by smearing them with ink.

'I can see nothing,' said I, handing it back to my friend.

'On the contrary, Watson, you can see everything. You fail, however, to reason from what you see. You are too timid in drawing your inferences.'

'Then, pray tell me what it is that you can infer from this hat?'

He picked it up and gazed at it in the peculiar introspective fashion which was characteristic of him. 'It is perhaps less suggestive than it might have been,' he remarked, 'and yet there are a few inferences which are very distinct, and a few others which represent at least a strong balance of probability. That the man was highly intellectual is of course obvious upon the face of it, and also that he was fairly well-to-do within the last three years, although he has now fallen upon evil days. He had foresight, but has less now than formerly, pointing to a moral retrogression, which, when taken with the decline of his fortunes, seems to indicate some evil influence, probably drink, at work upon him. This may account also for the obvious fact that his wife has ceased to love him.'

'My dear Holmes!'

'He has, however, retained some degree of self-respect,' he continued, disregarding my remonstrance. 'He is a man who leads a sedentary life, goes out little, is out of training entirely, is middle-aged, has grizzled hair which he has had cut within the last few days, and which he anoints with lime-cream. These are the more patent facts which are to be deduced from his hat. Also, by the way, that it is extremely improbable that he has gas laid on in his house.'

'You are certainly joking, Holmes.'

'Not in the least. Is it possible that even now, when I give you these results, you are unable to see how they are attained?'

'I have no doubt that I am very stupid, but I must confess that I am unable to follow you. For example, how did you deduce that this man was intellectual?'

For answer Holmes clapped the hat upon his head. It came right over the forehead and settled upon the bridge of his nose. 'It is a question of cubic capacity,' said he; 'a man with so large a brain must have something in it.'

'The decline of his fortunes, then?'

'This hat is three years old. These flat brims curled at the edge came in then. It is a hat of the very best quality. Look at the band of ribbed silk and the excellent lining. If this man could afford to buy so expensive a hat three years ago, and has had no hat since, then he has assuredly gone down in the world.'

'Well, that is clear enough, certainly. But how about the foresight and the moral retrogression?'

Sherlock Holmes laughed. 'Here is the foresight,' said he, putting his finger upon the little disc and loop of the hat-securer. 'They are never sold upon hats. If this man ordered one, it is a sign of a certain amount of foresight, since he went out of his way to take this precaution against the wind. But since we see that he has broken the elastic and has not troubled to replace it, it is obvious that he has less foresight now than formerly, which is a distinct proof of a weakening nature. On the other hand, he has endeavoured to conceal some of these stains upon the felt by daubing them with ink, which is a sign that he has not entirely lost his self-respect.'

'Your reasoning is certainly plausible.'

'The further points, that he is middle-aged, that his hair is grizzled, that it has been recently cut, and that he uses lime-cream, are all to be gathered from a close examination of the lower part of the lining. The lens discloses a large number of hair-ends, clean cut by the scissors of the barber. They all appear to be adhesive, and there is a distinct odour of lime-cream. This dust, you will observe, is not the gritty, gray dust of the street but the fluffy brown dust of the house, showing that it has been hung up indoors most of the time, while the marks of moisture upon the inside are proof positive that the wearer perspired very freely, and could therefore, hardly be in the best of training.'

'But his wife – you said that she had ceased to love him.'

'This hat has not been brushed for weeks. When I see you, my dear Watson, with a week's accumulation of dust upon your hat, and when your wife allows you to go out in such a state, I shall fear that you also have been unfortunate enough to lose your wife's affection.'

'But he might be a bachelor.'

'Nay, he was bringing home the goose as a peace-offering to his wife. Remember the card upon the bird's leg.'

'You have an answer to everything. But how on earth do you deduce that the gas is not laid on in his house?'

'One tallow stain, or even two, might come by chance; but when I see no less than five, I think that there can be little doubt that the individual must be brought into frequent contact with burning tallow – walks upstairs at night probably with his hat in one hand and a guttering candle in the other. Anyhow, he never got tallow-stains from a gasjet. Are you satisfied?'

'Well, it is very ingenious,' said I, laughing; 'but since, as you said just now, there has been no crime committed, and no harm done save the loss of a goose, all this seems to be rather a waste of energy.'

Sherlock Holmes had opened his mouth to reply, when the door flew open, and Peterson, the commissionaire, rushed into the apartment with flushed cheeks and the face of a man who is dazed with astonishment.

'The goose, Mr Holmes! The goose, sir!' he gasped.

'Eh? What of it, then? Has it returned to life and flapped off through the kitchen window?' Holmes twisted himself round upon the sofa to get a fairer view of the man's excited face.

'See here, sir! See what my wife found in its crop!' He held out his hand and displayed upon the centre of the palm a brilliantly scintillating blue stone, rather smaller than a bean in size, but of such purity and radiance that it twinkled like an electric point in the dark hollow of his hand.

Sherlock Holmes sat up with a whistle. 'By Jove, Peterson!' said he, 'this is treasure trove indeed. I suppose you know what you have got?'

'A diamond, sir? A precious stone. It cuts into glass as though it were putty.'

'It's more than a precious stone. It is *the* precious stone.'

'Not the Countess of Morcar's blue carbuncle!' I ejaculated.

'Precisely so. I ought to know its size and shape, seeing that I have read the advertisement about it in *The Times* every day lately. It is absolutely unique, and its value can only be conjectured, but the reward offered of £1000 is certainly not within a twentieth part of the market price.'

'A thousand pounds! Great Lord of mercy!' The commissionaire plumped down into a chair and stared from one to the other of us.

'That is the reward, and I have reason to know that there are sentimental considerations in the background which would induce the Countess to part with half her fortune if she could but recover the gem.'

'It was lost, if I remember aright, at the Hotel Cosmopolitan,' I remarked.

'Precisely so, on December 22d, just five days ago. John Horner, a plumber, was accused of having abstracted it from the lady's jewel-case. The evidence against him was so strong that the case has been referred to the Assizes. I have some account of the matter here, I believe.' He rummaged amid his newspapers, glancing over the dates, until at last he smoothed one out, doubled it over, and read the following paragraph:

'Hotel Cosmopolitan Jewel Robbery. John Horner, 26, plumber, was brought up upon the charge of having upon the 22d inst., abstracted from the jewel-case of the Countess of Morcar the valuable gem known as the blue carbuncle. James Ryder, upper-attendant at the hotel, gave his evidence to the effect that he had shown Horner up to the dressing-room of the Countess of Morcar upon the day of the robbery in order that he might solder the second bar of the grate, which was loose. He had remained with Horner some little time, but had finally been called away. On returning, he found that Horner had disappeared, that the bureau had been forced open, and that the small morocco casket in which, as it afterwards transpired, the Countess was accustomed to keep her jewel, was lying empty upon the dressing-table. Ryder instantly gave the alarm, and Horner was arrested the same evening; but the stone could not be found either upon his person or in his rooms. Catherine Cusack, maid to the Countess, deposed to having heard Ryder's cry of dismay on discovering the robbery, and to having rushed into the room, where she found matters as described by the last witness. Inspector Bradstreet, B division, gave evidence as to the arrest of Horner, who struggled frantically, and protested his innocence in the strongest terms. Evidence of a previous conviction for robbery having been given against the prisoner, the magistrate refused to deal summarily with the offence, but referred it to the Assizes. Horner, who had shown signs of intense emotion during the proceedings, fainted away at the conclusion and was carried out of court.

'Hum! So much for the police-court,' said Holmes thoughtfully, tossing aside the paper. 'The question for us now to solve is the sequence of events leading from a rifled jewel-case at one end to the crop of a goose in Tottenham Court Road at the other. You see, Watson, our little deductions have suddenly assumed a much more important and less innocent aspect. Here is the stone; the stone came from the goose, and the goose came from Mr Henry Baker, the gentleman with the bad hat and all the other characteristics with which I have bored you. So now we must set ourselves very seriously to finding this gentleman and ascertaining what part he has played in this little mystery. To do this, we must try the simplest means first, and these lie undoubtedly in an advertisement in all the evening papers. If this fail, I shall have recourse to other methods.'

'What will you say?'

'Give me a pencil and that slip of paper. Now, then:

'Found at the corner of Goodge Street, a goose and a black felt hat. Mr Henry Baker can have the same by applying at 6:30 this evening at 221B, Baker Street.

'That is clear and concise.'

'Very. But will he see it?'

'Well, he is sure to keep an eye on the papers, since, to a poor man, the loss was a heavy one. He was clearly so scared by his mischance in breaking the window and by the approach of Peterson that he thought of nothing but flight, but since then he must have bitterly regretted the impulse which caused him to drop his bird. Then, again, the introduction of his name will cause him to see it, for everyone who knows him will direct his attention to it. Here you are, Peterson, run down to the advertising agency and have this put in the evening papers.'

'In which, sir?'

'Oh, in the *Globe, Star, Pall Mall, St. James's, Evening News Standard, Echo,* and any others that occur to you.'

'Very well, sir. And this stone?'

'Ah, yes, I shall keep the stone. Thank you. And, I say, Peterson, just buy a goose on your way back and leave it here with me, for we must have one to give to this gentleman in place of the one which your family is now devouring.'

When the commissionaire had gone, Holmes took up the stone and held it against the light. 'It's a bonny thing,' said he. 'Just see how it glints and sparkles. Of course it is a nucleus and focus of crime. Every good stone is. They are the devil's pet baits. In the larger and older jewels every facet may stand for a bloody deed. This stone is not yet twenty years old. It was found in the banks of the Amoy River in southern China and is remarkable in having every characteristic of the carbuncle, save that it is blue in shade instead of ruby red. In spite of its youth, it has already a sinister history. There have been two murders, a vitriol-throwing, a suicide, and several robberies brought about for the sake of this forty-grain weight of crystallized charcoal. Who would think that so pretty a toy would be a purveyor to the gallows and the prison? I'll lock it up in my strong box now and drop a line to the Countess to say that we have it.'

'Do you think that this man Horner is innocent?'

'I cannot tell.'

'Well, then, do you imagine that this other one, Henry Baker, had anything to do with the matter?'

'It is, I think, much more likely that Henry Baker is an absolutely innocent man, who had no idea that the bird which he was carrying was of considerably more value than if it were made of solid gold. That, however, I shall determine by a very simple test if we have an answer to our advertisement.'

'And you can do nothing until then?'

'Nothing.'

'In that case I shall continue my professional round. But I shall come back in the evening at the hour you have mentioned, for I should like to see the solution of so tangled a business.'

'Very glad to see you. I dine at seven. There is a woodcock, I believe. By the way, in view of recent occurrences, perhaps I ought to ask Mrs Hudson to examine its crop.'

I had been delayed at a case, and it was a little after half-past six when I found myself in Baker Street once more. As I approached the house I saw a tall man in a Scotch bonnet with a coat which was buttoned up to his chin waiting outside in the bright semicircle which was thrown from the fanlight. Just as I arrived the door was opened, and we were shown up together to Holmes's room.

'Mr Henry Baker, I believe,' said he, rising from his armchair and greeting his visitor with the easy air of geniality which he could so readily assume. 'Pray take this chair by the fire, Mr Baker. It is a cold night, and I observe that your circulation is more adapted for summer than for winter. Ah, Watson, you have just come at the right time. Is that your hat, Mr Baker?'

'Yes, sir, that is undoubtedly my hat.'

He was a large man with rounded shoulders, a massive head, and a broad, intelligent face, sloping down to a pointed beard of grizzled brown. A touch of red in nose and cheeks, with a slight tremor of his extended hand, recalled Holmes's surmise as to his habits. His rusty black frock-coat was buttoned right up in front, with the collar turned up, and his lank wrists protruded from his sleeves without a sign of cuff or shirt. He spoke in a slow staccato fashion, choosing his words with care, and gave the impression generally of a man of learning and letters who had had ill-usage at the hands of fortune.

'We have retained these things for some days,' said Holmes, 'because we expected to see an advertisement from you giving your address. I am at a loss to know now why you did not advertise.'

Our visitor gave a rather shamefaced laugh. 'Shillings have not been so plentiful with me as they once were,' he remarked. 'I had no doubt that the gang of roughs who assaulted me had carried off both my hat and the bird. I did not care to spend more money in a hopeless attempt at recovering them.'

'Very naturally. By the way, about the bird, we were compelled to eat it.'

'To eat it!' Our visitor half rose from his chair in his excitement.

'Yes, it would have been of no use to anyone had we not done so. But I presume that this other goose upon the sideboard, which is about the same weight and perfectly fresh, will answer your purpose equally well?'

'Oh, certainly, certainly,' answered Mr Baker with a sigh of relief.

'Of course, we still have the feathers, legs, crop, and so on of your own bird, so if you wish – '

The man burst into a hearty laugh. 'They might be useful to me as relics of my adventure,' said he, 'but beyond that I can hardly see what use the *disjecta membra* of my late acquaintance are going to be to me. No, sir, I think that, with your permission, I will confine my attentions to the excellent bird which I perceive upon the sideboard.'

Sherlock Holmes glanced sharply across at me with a slight shrug of his shoulders.

'There is your hat, then, and there your bird,' said he. 'By the way, would it bore you to tell me where you got the other one from? I am somewhat of a fowl fancier, and I have seldom seen a better grown goose.'

'Certainly, sir,' said Baker, who had risen and tucked his newly gained property under his arm. 'There are a few of us who frequent the Alpha Inn, near the Museum – we are to be found in the Museum itself during the day, you understand. This year our good host, Windigate by name, instituted a goose club, by which, on consideration of some few pence every week, we were each to receive a bird at Christmas. My pence were duly paid, and the rest is familiar to you. I am much indebted to you, sir, for a Scotch bonnet is fitted neither to my years nor my gravity.' With a comical pomposity of manner he bowed solemnly to both of us and strode off upon his way.

'So much for Mr Henry Baker,' said Holmes when he had closed the door behind him. 'It is quite certain that he knows nothing whatever about the matter. Are you hungry, Watson?'

'Not particularly.'

'Then I suggest that we turn our dinner into a supper and follow up this clue while it is still hot.'

'By all means.

It was a bitter night, so we drew on our ulsters and wrapped cravats about our throats. Outside, the stars were shining coldly in a cloudless sky, and the breath of the passers-by blew out into smoke like so many pistol shots. Our footfalls rang out crisply and loudly as we swung through the doctors' quarter, Wimpole Street, Harley Street, and so through Wigmore Street into Oxford Street. In a quarter of an hour we were in Bloomsbury at the Alpha Inn, which is a small public-house at the corner of one of the streets which runs down into Holborn. Holmes pushed open the door of the private bar and ordered two glasses of beer from the ruddy-faced, white-aproned landlord.

'Your beer should be excellent if it is as good as your geese,' said he.

'My geese!' The man seemed surprised.

'Yes. I was speaking only half an hour ago to Mr Henry Baker, who was a member of your goose club.'

'Ah! yes, I see. But you see, sir, them's not our geese.'

'Indeed! Whose, then?'

'Well, I got the two dozen from a salesman in Covent Garden.'

'Indeed? I know some of them. Which was it?'

'Breckinridge is his name.'

'Ah! I don't know him. Well, here's your good health landlord, and prosperity to your house. Good-night.'

'Now for Mr Breckinridge,' he continued, buttoning up his coat as we came out into the frosty air. 'Remember, Watson that though we have so homely a thing as a goose at one end of this chain, we have at the other a man who will certainly get seven years' penal servitude unless we can establish his innocence. It is possible that our inquiry may but confirm his guilt but, in any case, we have a line of investigation which has been missed by the police, and which a singular chance has placed in our hands. Let us follow it out to the bitter end. Faces to the south, then, and quick march!'

We passed across Holborn, down Endell Street, and so through a zigzag of slums to Covent Garden Market. One of the largest stalls bore the name of Breckinridge upon it, and the proprietor a horsy-looking man, with a sharp face and trim side-whiskers was helping a boy to put up the shutters.

'Good-evening. It's a cold night,' said Holmes.

The salesman nodded and shot a questioning glance at my companion.

'Sold out of geese, I see,' continued Holmes, pointing at the bare slabs of marble.

'Let you have five hundred to-morrow morning.'

'That's no good.'

'Well, there are some on the stall with the gas-flare.'

'Ah, but I was recommended to you.'

'Who by?'

'The landlord of the Alpha.'

'Oh, yes; I sent him a couple of dozen.'

'Fine birds they were, too. Now where did you get them from?'

To my surprise the question provoked a burst of anger from the salesman.

'Now, then, mister,' said he, with his head cocked and his arms akimbo, 'what are you driving at? Let's have it straight, now.'

'It is straight enough. I should like to know who sold you the geese which you supplied to the Alpha.'

'Well then, I shan't tell you. So now!'

'Oh, it is a matter of no importance; but I don't know why you should be so warm over such a trifle.'

'Warm! You'd be as warm, maybe, if you were as pestered as I am. When I pay good money for a good article there should be an end of the business; but it's "Where are the geese?" and "Who did you sell the geese to?" and "What will you take for the geese?" One would think they were the only geese in the world, to hear the fuss that is made over them.'

'Well, I have no connection with any other people who have been making inquiries,' said Holmes carelessly. 'If you won't tell us the bet is off, that is all. But I'm always ready to back my opinion on a matter of fowls, and I have a fiver on it that the bird I ate is country bred.'

'Well, then, you've lost your fiver, for it's town bred,' snapped the salesman.

'It's nothing of the kind.'

'I say it is.'

'I don't believe it.'

'D'you think you know more about fowls than I, who have handled them ever since I was a nipper? I tell you, all those birds that went to the Alpha were town bred.'

'You'll never persuade me to believe that.'

'Will you bet, then?'

'It's merely taking your money, for I know that I am right. But I'll have a sovereign on with you, just to teach you not to be obstinate.'

The salesman chuckled grimly. 'Bring me the books, Bill,' said he.

The small boy brought round a small thin volume and a great greasy-backed one, laying them out together beneath the hanging lamp.

'Now then, Mr Cocksure,' said the salesman, 'I thought that I was out of geese, but before I finish you'll find that there is still one left in my shop. You see this little book?'

'Well?'

'That's the list of the folk from whom I buy. D'you see? Well, then, here on this page are the country folk, and the numbers after their names are where their accounts are in the big ledger. Now, then! You see this other page in red ink? Well, that is a list of my town suppliers. Now, look at that third name. Just read it out to me.'

'Mrs Oakshott, 117, Brixton Road – 249,' read Holmes.

'Quite so. Now turn that up in the ledger.'

Holmes turned to the page indicated. 'Here you are, "Mrs Oakshott, 117, Brixton Road, egg and poultry supplier." '

'Now, then, what's the last entry?'

' "December 22d. Twenty-four geese at 7*s*. 6*d*." '

'Quite so. There you are. And underneath?'

' "Sold to Mr Windigate of the Alpha, at 12*s*. " '

'What have you to say now?'

Sherlock Holmes looked deeply chagrined. He drew a sovereign from his pocket and threw it down upon the slab, turning away with the air of a man whose disgust is too deep for words. A few yards off he stopped under a lamp-post and laughed in the hearty, noiseless fashion which was peculiar to him.

'When you see a man with whiskers of that cut and the "Pink 'un" protruding out of his pocket, you can always draw him by a bet,' said he. 'I daresay that if I had put £100 down in front of him, that man would not have given me such complete information as was drawn from him by the idea that he was doing me on a wager. Well, Watson, we are, I fancy, nearing the end of our quest, and the only point which remains to be determined is whether we should go on to this Mrs Oakshott to-night, or whether we should reserve it for to-morrow. It is clear from what that surly fellow said that there are others besides ourselves who are anxious about the matter, and I should – '

His remarks were suddenly cut short by a loud hubbub which broke out from the stall which we had just left. Turning round we saw a little rat-faced fellow standing in the centre of the circle of yellow light which was thrown by the swinging lamp, while Breckinridge, the salesman, framed in the door of his stall, was shaking his fists fiercely at the cringing figure.

'I've had enough of you and your geese,' he shouted. 'I wish you were all at the devil together. If you come pestering me any more with your silly talk I'll set the dog at you. You bring Mrs Oakshott here and I'll answer her, but what have you to do with it? Did I buy the geese off you?'

'No; but one of them was mine all the same,' whined the little man.

'Well, then, ask Mrs Oakshott for it.'

'She told me to ask you.'

'Well, you can ask the King of Proosia, for all I care. I've had enough of it. Get out of this!' He rushed fiercely forward, and the inquirer flitted away into the darkness.

'Ha! this may save us a visit to Brixton Road,' whispered Holmes. 'Come with me, and we will see what is to be made of this fellow.' Striding through the scattered knots of people who lounged round the flaring stalls, my companion speedily overtook the little man and touched him upon the shoulder. He sprang round, and I could see in the gas-light that every vestige of colour had been driven from his face.

'Who are you, then? What do you want?' he asked in a quavering voice.

'You will excuse me,' said Holmes blandly, 'but I could not help overhearing the questions which you put to the salesman just now. I think that I could be of assistance to you.'

'You? Who are you? How could you know anything of the matter?'

'My name is Sherlock Holmes. It is my business to know what other people don't know.'

'But you can know nothing of this?'

'Excuse me, I know everything of it. You are endeavouring to trace some geese which were sold by Mrs Oakshott, of Brixton Road, to a salesman named Breckinridge, by him in turn to Mr Windigate, of the Alpha, and by him to his club, of which Mr Henry Baker is a member.'

'Oh, sir, you are the very man whom I have longed to meet,' cried the little fellow with outstretched hands and quivering fingers. 'I can hardly explain to you how interested I am in this matter.'

Sherlock Holmes hailed a four-wheeler which was passing. 'In that case we had better discuss it in a cosy room rather than in this wind-swept market-place,' said he. 'But pray tell me, before we go farther, who it is that I have the pleasure of assisting.'

The man hesitated for an instant. 'My name is John Robinson,' he answered with a sidelong glance.

'No, no; the real name,' said Holmes sweetly. 'It is always awkward doing business with an alias.'

A flush sprang to the white cheeks of the stranger. 'Well then,' said he, 'my real name is James Ryder.'

'Precisely so. Head attendant at the Hotel Cosmopolitan. Pray step into the cab, and I shall soon be able to tell you everything which you would wish to know.'

The little man stood glancing from one to the other of us with half-frightened, half-hopeful eyes, as one who is not sure whether he is on the verge of a windfall or of a catastrophe. Then he stepped into the cab, and in half an hour we were back in the sitting-room at Baker Street. Nothing had been said during our drive, but the high, thin breathing of our new companion, and the claspings and unclaspings of his hands, spoke of the nervous tension within him.

'Here we are!' said Holmes cheerily as we filed into the room. 'The fire looks very seasonable in this weather. You look cold, Mr Ryder. Pray take the basket-chair. I will just put on my slippers before we settle this little matter of yours. Now, then! You want to know what became of those geese?'

'Yes, sir.'

'Or rather, I fancy, of that goose. It was one bird, I imagine in which you were interested – white, with a black bar across the tail.'

Ryder quivered with emotion. 'Oh, sir,' he cried, 'can you tell me where it went to?'

'It came here.'

'Here?'

'Yes, and a most remarkable bird it proved. I don't

wonder that you should take an interest in it. It laid an egg after it was dead – the bonniest, brightest little blue egg that ever was seen. I have it here in my museum.'

'Our visitor staggered to his feet and clutched the mantelpiece with his right hand. Holmes unlocked his strong-box and held up the blue carbuncle, which shone out like a star, with a cold, brilliant, many-pointed radiance. Ryder stood glaring with a drawn face, uncertain whether to claim or to disown it.

'The game's up, Ryder,' said Holmes quietly. 'Hold up, man, or you'll be into the fire! Give him an arm back into his chair, Watson. He's not got blood enough to go in for felony with impunity. Give him a dash of brandy. So! Now he looks a little more human. What a shrimp it is, to be sure!'

For a moment he had staggered and nearly fallen, but the brandy brought a tinge of colour into his cheeks, and he sat staring with frightened eyes at his accuser.

'I have almost every link in my hands, and all the proofs which I could possibly need, so there is little which you need tell me. Still, that little may as well be cleared up to make the case complete. You had heard, Ryder, of this blue stone of the Countess of Morcar's?'

'It was Catherine Cusack who told me of it,' said he in a crackling voice.

'I see – her ladyship's waiting-maid. Well, the temptation of sudden wealth so easily acquired was too much for you, as it has been for better men before you; but you were not very scrupulous in the means you used. It seems to me, Ryder, that there is the making of a very pretty villain in you. You knew that this man Horner, the plumber, had been concerned in some such matter before, and that suspicion would rest the more readily upon him. What did you do, then? You made some small job in my lady's room – you and your confederate Cusack – and you managed that he should be the man sent for. Then, when he had left, you rifled the jewel-case, raised the alarm, and had this unfortunate man arrested. You then – '

Ryder threw himself down suddenly upon the rug and clutched at my companion's knees. 'For God's sake, have mercy!' he shrieked. 'Think of my father! of my mother! It would break their hearts. I never went wrong before! I never will again. I swear it. I'll swear it on a Bible. Oh, don't bring it into court! For Christ's sake, don't!'

'Get back into your chair!' said Holmes sternly. 'It is very well to cringe and crawl now, but you thought little enough of this poor Horner in the dock for a crime of which he knew nothing.'

'I will fly, Mr Holmes. I will leave the country, sir. Then the charge against him will break down.'

'Hum! We will talk about that. And now let us hear a true account of the next act. How came the stone into the goose, and how came the goose into the open market? Tell us the truth, for there lies your only hope of safety.'

Ryder passed his tongue over his parched lips. 'I will tell you it just as it happened, sir,' said he. 'When Horner had been arrested, it seemed to me that it would be best for me to get away with the stone at once, for I did not know at what moment the police might not take it into their heads to search me and my room. There was no place about the hotel where it would be safe. I went out, as if on some commission, and I made for my sister's house. She had married a man named Oakshott, and lived in Brixton Road, where she fattened fowls for the market. All the way there every man I met seemed to me to be a policeman or a detective; and, for all that it was a cold night, the sweat was pouring down my face before I came to the Brixton Road. My sister asked me what was the matter, and why I was so pale; but I told her that I had been upset by the jewel robbery at the hotel. Then I went into the back yard and smoked a pipe and wondered what it would be best to do.

'I had a friend once called Maudsley, who went to the bad, and has just been serving his time in Pentonville. One day he had met me, and fell into talk about the ways of thieves, and how they could get rid of what they stole. I knew that he would be true to me, for I knew one or two things about him; so I made up my mind to go right on to Kilburn, where he lived, and take him into my confidence. He would show me how to turn the stone into money. But how to get to him in safety? I thought of the agonies I had gone through in coming from the hotel. I might at any moment be seized and searched, and there would be the stone in my waistcoat pocket. I was leaning against the wall at the time and looking at the geese which were waddling about round my feet, and suddenly an idea came into my head which showed me how I could beat the best detective that ever lived.

'My sister had told me some weeks before that I might have the pick of her geese for a Christmas present, and I knew that she was always as good as her word. I would take my goose now, and in it I would carry my stone to Kilburn. There was a little shed in the yard, and behind this I drove one of the birds – a fine big one, white, with a barred tail. I caught it, and prying its bill open, I thrust the stone down its throat as far as my finger could reach. The bird gave a gulp, and I felt the stone pass along its gullet and down into its crop. But the creature flapped and struggled, and out came my sister to know what was the matter. As I turned to speak to her the brute broke loose and fluttered off among the others.

' "Whatever were you doing with that bird, Jem?" says she.

' "Well," said I, "you said you'd give me one for Christmas, and I was feeling which was the fattest."

' "Oh," says she, "we've set yours aside for you – Jem's bird, we call it. It's the big white one over yonder. There's twenty-six of them, which makes one for you, and one for us, and two dozen for the market."

' "Thank you, Maggie," says I; "but if it is all the same to you, I'd rather have that one I was handling just now."

' "The other is a good three pound heavier," said she, "and we fattened it expressly for you."

' "Never mind. I'll have the other, and I'll take it now," said I.

' "Oh, just as you like," said she, a little huffed. "Which is it you want, then?"

' "That white one with the barred tail, right in the middle of the flock."

' "Oh, very well. Kill it and take it with you."

'Well, I did what she said, Mr Holmes, and I carried the bird all the way to Kilburn. I told my pal what I had done, for he was a man that it was easy to tell a thing like that to. He laughed until he choked, and we got a knife and opened the goose. My heart turned to water, for there was no sign of the stone, and I knew that some terrible mistake had occurred. I left the bird, rushed back to my sister's, and hurried into the back yard. There was not a bird to be seen there.

' "Where are they all, Maggie?" I cried.

' "Gone to the dealer's, Jem."

' "Which dealer's?"

' "Breckinridge, of Covent Garden."

' "But was there another with a barred tail?" I asked, "the same as the one I chose?"

' "Yes, Jem; there were two barred-tailed ones, and I could never tell them apart."

'Well, then, of course I saw it all, and I ran off as hard as my feet would carry me to this man Breckinridge; but he had sold the lot at once, and not one word would he tell me as to where they had gone. You heard him yourselves to-night. Well, he has always answered me like that. My sister thinks that I am going mad. Sometimes I think that I am myself. And now – and now I am myself a branded thief, without ever having touched the wealth for which I sold my character. God help me! God help me!' He burst into convulsive sobbing, with his face buried in his hands.

There was a long silence, broken only by his heavy breathing and by the measured tapping of Sherlock Holmes's finger-tips upon the edge of the table. Then my friend rose and threw open the door.

'Get out!' said he.

'What, sir! Oh, Heaven bless you!'

'No more words. Get out!'

And no more words were needed. There was a rush, a clatter upon the stairs, the bang of a door, and the crisp rattle of running footfalls from the street.

'After all, Watson,' said Holmes, reaching up his hand for his clay pipe, 'I am not retained by the police to supply their deficiencies. If Horner were in danger it would be another thing; but this fellow will not appear against him, and the case must collapse. I suppose that I am commuting a felony, but it is just possible that I am saving a soul. This fellow will not go wrong again; he is too terribly frightened. Send him to jail now, and you make him a jail-bird for life. Besides, it is the season of forgiveness. Chance has put in our way a most singular and whimsical problem, and its solution is its own reward. If you will have the goodness to touch the bell, Doctor, we will begin another investigation, in which, also a bird will be the chief feature.'

Pip's Christmas

from *Great Expectations*

Charles Dickens

The story so far:

Pip, a young orphan, lives with his older sister and her husband Joe Gargery, the local blacksmith.

While Joe says he and Pip are 'ever the best of friends', Pip's sister ('Mrs Joe') has considerably fewer warm feelings towards him.

Just before this chapter opens, Pip meets an escaped convict, Magwitch, on the marshes. Magwitch terrifies Pip into stealing food for him, threatening him with dismemberment by his companion, an (imaginary) young man. Pip takes Magwitch some of the best bits of the family's impending Christmas dinner, including some brandy; he hides the theft by topping up the brandy bottle with tar-water. To this Christmas dinner, Mrs Joe's ghastly friends have been invited.

Pip waits on tenterhooks to be discovered...

I fully expected to find a Constable in the kitchen, waiting to take me up. But not only was there no Constable there, but no discovery had yet been made of the robbery. Mrs Joe was prodigiously busy in getting the house ready for the festivities of the day, and Joe had been put upon the kitchen doorstep to keep him out of the dust-pan, – an article into which his destiny always led him, sooner or later, when my sister was vigorously reaping the floors of her establishment.

'And where the deuce ha' *you* been?' was Mrs Joe's Christmas salutation, when I and my conscience showed ourselves.

I said I had been down to hear the Carols. 'Ah! well!' observed Mrs Joe. 'You might ha' done worse.' Not a doubt of that, I thought.

'Perhaps if I warn't a blacksmith's wife, and (what's the same thing) a slave with her apron never off, *I* should have been to hear the Carols,' said Mrs Joe. 'I'm rather partial to Carols, myself, and that's the best of reasons for my never hearing any.'

Joe, who had ventured into the kitchen after me as the dustpan had retired before us, drew the back of his hand across his nose with a conciliatory air, when Mrs Joe darted a look at him, and, when her eyes were withdrawn, secretly crossed his two forefingers, and exhibited them to me, as our token that Mrs Joe was in a cross temper. This was so much her normal state, that Joe and I would often, for weeks together, be, as to our fingers, like monumental Crusaders as to their legs.

We were to have a superb dinner, consisting of a leg of pickled pork and greens, and a pair of roast stuffed fowls. A handsome mince-pie had been made yesterday morning (which accounted for the mincemeat not being missed), and the pudding was already on the boil. These extensive arrangements occasioned us to be cut off unceremoniously in respect of breakfast; 'for I ain't,' said Mrs. Joe, – 'I ain't a going to have no formal cramming and busting and washing up now, with what I've got before me, I promise you!'

So, we had our slices served out, as if we were two thousand troops on a forced march instead of a man and boy at home; and we took gulps of milk and water, with apologetic countenances, from a jug on the dresser. In the meantime, Mrs Joe put clean white curtains up, and tacked a new flowered flounce across the wide chimney to replace the old one, and uncovered the little state parlour across the passage, which was never uncovered at any other time, but passed the rest of the year in a cool haze of silver paper, which even extended to the four little white crockery poodles on the mantel-shelf, each with a black nose and a basket of flowers in his mouth, and each the counterpart of the other. Mrs Joe was a very clean housekeeper, but had an exquisite art of making her cleanliness more uncomfortable and unacceptable than dirt itself. Cleanliness is next to Godliness, and some people do the same by their religion.

My sister, having so much to do, was going to church vicariously, that is to say, Joe and I were going. In his working-clothes, Joe was a well-knit characteristic-looking blacksmith; in his holiday clothes, he was more like a scarecrow in good circumstances, than anything else. Nothing that he wore then fitted him or seemed to belong to him; and everything that he wore then grazed him. On the present festive occasion he emerged from his room, when the blithe bells were going, the picture of misery, in a full suit of Sunday penitentials. As to me, I think my sister must have had some general idea that I was a young offender whom an Accoucheur Policeman had taken up (on my birthday) and delivered over to her, to be dealt with according to the outraged majesty of the law. I was always treated as if I had insisted on being born in opposition to the dictates of reason, religion, and morality, and against the dissuading arguments of my best friends. Even when I was taken to have a new suit of clothes, the tailor had orders to make them like a kind of Reformatory, and on no account to let me have the free use of my limbs. Joe and I going to church, therefore, must have been a moving spectacle for compassionate minds. Yet, what I suffered outside was nothing to what I underwent within. The terrors that had assailed me whenever Mrs Joe had gone near the pantry, or out of the room, were only to be equalled by the remorse with which my mind dwelt on what my hands had done. Under the weight of my wicked secret, I pondered whether the Church would be powerful enough to shield me from the vengeance of the terrible young man, if I divulged to that establishment. I conceived the idea that the time when the banns were read and when the clergyman said, 'Ye are now to declare it!' would be the time for me to rise and propose a private conference in the vestry. I am far from being sure that I might not have astonished our small congregation by resorting to this extreme measure, but for its being Christmas Day and no Sunday.

Mr Wopsle, the clerk at church, was to dine with us; and Mr Hubble the wheelwright and Mrs. Hubble; and Uncle Pumblechook (Joe's uncle, but Mrs Joe appropriated him), who was a well-to-do cornchandler in the nearest town, and drove his own chaise-cart. The dinner hour was half-past one. When Joe and I got home, we found the table laid, and Mrs Joe dressed, and the dinner dressing, and the front door unlocked (it never was at any other time) for the company to enter by, and everything most splendid. And still, not a word of the robbery.

The time came, without bringing with it any relief to my feelings, and the company came. Mr Wopsle, united to a Roman nose and a large shining bald forehead, had a deep voice which he was uncommonly proud of; indeed it was understood among his acquaintance that if you could only give him his head, he would read the clergyman into fits; he himself confessed that if the Church was 'thrown open,' meaning to competition, he would not despair of making his mark in it. The Church not being 'thrown open,' he was, as I have said, our clerk. But he punished the Amens tremendously; and when he gave out the psalm – always giving the whole verse – he looked all round the congregation first, as much as to say, 'You have heard my friend overhead; oblige me with your opinion of this style!'

I opened the door to the company – making believe that it was a habit of ours to open that door – and I opened it

36

first to Mr Wopsle, next to Mr and Mrs Hubble, and last of all to Uncle Pumblechook. N.B. *I* was not allowed to call him uncle, under the severest penalties.

'Mrs Joe,' said Uncle Pumblechook, a large hard-breathing middle-aged slow man, with a mouth like a fish, dull staring eyes, and sandy hair standing upright on his head, so that he looked as if he had just been all but choked, and had that moment come to, 'I have brought you as the compliments of the season – I have brought you, Mum, a bottle of sherry wine – and I have brought you, Mum, a bottle of port wine.'

Every Christmas Day he presented himself, as a profound novelty, with exactly the same words, and carrying the two bottles like dumb-bells. Every Christmas Day, Mrs Joe replied, as she now replied, 'O, Un-cle Pumble-chook! This IS kind!' Every Christmas Day, he retorted, as he now retorted, 'It's no more than your merits. And now are you all bobbish, and how's Sixpennorth of halfpence?' meaning me.

We dined on these occasions in the kitchen, and adjourned, for the nuts and oranges and apples to the parlour; which was a change very like Joe's change from his working-clothes to his Sunday dress. My sister was uncommonly lively on the present occasion, and indeed was generally more gracious in the society of Mrs Hubble than in other company. I remember Mrs Hubble as a little curly sharp-edged person in sky-blue, who held a conventionally juvenile position, because she had married Mr Hubble – I don't know at what remote period – when she was much younger than he. I remember Mr Hubble as a tough, high-shouldered, stooping old man, of a sawdusty fragrance, with his legs extraordinarily wide apart: so that in my short days I always saw some miles of open country between them when I met him coming up the lane.

Among this good company I should have felt myself, even if I hadn't robbed the pantry, in a false position. Not because I was squeezed in at an acute angle of the tablecloth, with the table in my chest, and the Pumblechookian elbow in my eye, nor because I was not allowed to speak (I didn't want to speak), nor because I was regaled with the scaly tips of the drumsticks of the fowls, and with those obscure corners of pork of which the pig, when living, had had the least reason to be vain. No; I should not have minded that, if they would only have left me alone. But they wouldn't leave me alone. They seemed to think the opportunity lost, if they failed to point the conversation at me, every now and then, and stick the point into me. I might have been an unfortunate little bull in a Spanish arena, I got so smartingly touched up by these moral goads.

It began the moment we sat down to dinner. Mr Wopsle said grace with theatrical declamation – as it now appears to me, something like a religious cross of the Ghost in Hamlet with Richard the Third – and ended with the very proper aspiration that we might be truly grateful. Upon which my sister fixed me with her eye, and said, in a low reproachful voice, 'Do you hear that? Be grateful.'

'Especially,' said Mr Pumblechook, 'be grateful, boy, to them which brought you up by hand.'

Mrs Hubble shook her head, and contemplating me with a mournful presentiment that I should come to no good, asked, 'Why is it that the young are never grateful?' This moral mystery seemed too much for the company until Mr Hubble tersely solved it by saying, 'Naterally wicious.' Everybody then murmured 'True!' and looked at me in a particularly unpleasant and personal manner.

Joe's station and influence were something feebler (if possible) when there was company than when there was none. But he always aided and comforted me when he could, in some way of his own, and he always did so at dinner-time by giving me gravy, if there were any. There being plenty of gravy to-day, Joe spooned into my plate, at this point, about half a pint.

A little later on in the dinner, Mr Wopsle reviewed the sermon with some severity, and intimated – in the usual hypothetical case of the Church being 'thrown open' – what kind of sermon he would have given them. After favouring them with some heads of that discourse, he remarked that he considered the subject of the day's homily, ill chosen; which was the less excusable, he added, when there were so many subjects 'going about.'

'True again,' said Uncle Pumblechook. 'You've hit it, sir! Plenty of subjects going about, for them that know how to put salt upon their tails. That's what's wanted. A man needn't go far to find a subject, if he's ready with his salt-box.' Mr Pumblechook added, after a short interval of reflection, 'Look at Pork alone. There's a subject! If you want a subject, look at Pork!'

'True, sir. Many a moral for the young,' returned Mr Wopsle, – and I knew he was going to lug me in, before he said it; 'might be deduced from that text.'

('You listen to this,' said my sister to me, in a severe parenthesis.)

Joe gave me some more gravy.

'Swine,' pursued Mr. Wopsle, in his deepest voice, and pointing his fork at my blushes, as if he were mentioning my Christian name, – 'swine were the companions of the prodigal. The gluttony of Swine is put before us, as an example to the young.' (I thought this pretty well in him who had been praising up the pork for being so plump and juicy.) 'What is detestable in a pig is more detestable in a boy.'

'Or girl,' suggested Mr Hubble.

'Of course, or girl, Mr Hubble,' assented Mr Wopsle, rather irritably, 'but there is no girl present.'

'Besides,' said Mr Pumblechook, turning sharp on me, 'think what you've got to be grateful for. If you'd been born a Squeaker –'

'He *was*, if ever a child was,' said my sister, most emphatically.

Joe gave me some more gravy.

'Well, but I mean a four-footed Squeaker,' said Mr Pumblechook. 'If you had been born such, would you have been here now? Not you —'

'Unless in that form,' said Mr Wopsle, nodding towards the dish.

'But I don't mean in that form, sir,' returned Mr Pumblechook, who had an objection to being interrupted; 'I mean, enjoying himself with his elders and betters, and improving himself with their conversation, and rolling in the lap of luxury. Would he have been doing that? No, he wouldn't. And what would have been your destination?' turning on me again. 'You would have been disposed of for so many shillings according to the market price of the article, and Dunstable the butcher would have come up to you as you lay in your straw, and he would have whipped you under his left arm, and with his right he would have tucked up his frock to get a penknife from out of his waistcoat-pocket, and he would have shed your blood and had your life. No bringing up by hand then. Not a bit of it!'

Joe offered me more gravy, which I was afraid to take.

'He was a world of trouble to you, ma'am,' said Mrs Hubble, commiserating my sister.

'Trouble?' echoed my sister; 'trouble?' and then entered on a fearful catalogue of all the illnesses I had been guilty of, and all the acts of sleeplessness I had committed, and all the high places I had tumbled from, and all the low places I had tumbled into, and all the injuries I had done myself, and all the times she had wished me in my grave, and I had contumaciously refused to go there.

I think the Romans must have aggravated one another very much, with their noses. Perhaps, they became the restless people they were, in consequence. Anyhow, Mr

Wopsle's Roman nose so aggravated me, during the recital of my misdemeanours, that I should have liked to pull it until he howled. But, all I had endured up to this time was nothing in comparison with the awful feelings that took possession of me when the pause was broken which ensued upon my sister's recital, and in which pause everybody had looked at me (as I felt painfully conscious) with indignation and abhorrence.

'Yet,' said Mr. Pumblechook, leading the company gently back to the theme from which they had strayed, ' Pork – regarded as biled – is rich, too; ain't it?'

'Have a little brandy, uncle,' said my sister.

O Heavens, it had come at last! He would find it was weak, he would say it was weak, and I was lost! I held tight to the leg of the table under the cloth, with both hands, and awaited my fate.

My sister went for the stone bottle, came back with the stone bottle, and poured his brandy out: no one else taking any. The wretched man trifled with his glass, – took it up, looked at it through the light, put it down, – prolonged my misery. All this time Mrs Joe and Joe were briskly clearing the table for the pie and pudding.

I couldn't keep my eyes off him. Always holding tight by the leg of the table with my hands and feet, I saw the miserable creature finger his glass playfully, take it up, smile, throw his head back, and drink the brandy off. Instantly afterwards, the company were seized with unspeakable consternation, owing to his springing to his feet, turning round several times in an appalling spasmodic whooping-cough dance, and rushing out at the door; he then became visible through the window, violently plunging and expectorating, making the most hideous faces, and apparently out of his mind.

I held on tight, while Mrs Joe and Joe ran to him. I didn't know how I had done it, but I had no doubt I had murdered him somehow. In my dreadful situation, it was a relief when he was brought back, and surveying the company all round as if *they* had disagreed with him, sank down into his chair with the one significant gasp, 'Tar!'

I had filled up the bottle from the tar-water jug. I knew he would be worse by and by. I moved the table, like a Medium of the present day, by the vigour of my unseen hold upon it.

'Tar!' cried my sister, in amazement. 'Why, how ever could Tar come there?'

But, Uncle Pumblechook, who was omnipotent in that kitchen, wouldn't hear the word, wouldn't hear of the subject, imperiously waved it all away with his hand, and asked for hot gin and water. My sister, who had begun to be alarmingly meditative, had to employ herself actively in getting the gin, the hot water, the sugar, and the lemon-peel, and mixing them. For the time being at least, I was saved. I still held on to the leg of the table, but clutched it now with the fervour of gratitude.

By degrees, I became calm enough to release my grasp and partake of pudding. Mr Pumblechook partook of pudding. All partook of pudding. The course terminated, and Mr. Pumblechook had begun to beam under the genial influence of gin and water. I began to think I should get over the day, when my sister said to Joe, 'Clean plates – cold.'

I clutched the leg of the table again immediately, and pressed it to my bosom as if it had been the companion of my youth and friend of my soul. I foresaw what was coming, and I felt that this time I really was gone.

'You must taste,' said my sister, addressing the guests with her best grace, 'you must taste, to finish with, such a delightful and delicious present of Uncle Pumblechook's!'

Must they! Let them not hope to taste it!

'You must know,' said my sister, rising, 'it's a pie; a savoury pork pie.'

The company murmured their compliments. Uncle

Pumblechook, sensible of having deserved well of his fellow-creatures, said, – quite vivaciously, all things considered, – 'Well, Mrs Joe, we'll do our best endeavours; let us have a cut at this same pie.'

My sister went out to get it. I heard her steps proceed to the pantry. I saw Mr Pumblechook balance his knife. I saw reawakening appetite in the Roman nostrils of Mr Wopsle. I heard Mr Hubble remark that 'a bit of savoury pork pie would lay atop of anything you could mention, and do no harm,' and I heard Joe say, 'You shall have some, Pip.' I have never been absolutely certain whether I uttered a shrill yell of terror, merely in spirit, or in the bodily hearing of the company. I felt that I could bear no more, and that I must run away. I released the leg of the table, and ran for my life.

But I ran no farther than the house door, for there I ran head-foremost into a party of soldiers with their muskets, one of whom held out a pair of handcuffs to me, saying, 'Here you are, look sharp, come on!'

Christmas Day at Kirkby Cottage

Anthony Trollope

Like Dickens, Trollope produced a great many Christmas stories. Christmas Day at Kirkby Cottage *was originally published in* Routledge's Christmas Annual *in 1870.*

What Maurice Archer Said about Christmas

'After all, Christmas is a bore!'

'Even though you should think so, Mr Archer, pray do not say so here.'

'But it is.'

'I am very sorry that you should feel like that; but pray do not say anything so very horrible.'

'Why not? and why is it horrible? You know very well what I mean.'

'I do not want to know what you mean; and it would make papa very unhappy if he were to hear you.'

'A great deal of beef is roasted, and a great deal of pudding is boiled, and then people try to be jolly by eating more than usual. The consequence is, they get very sleepy, and want to go to bed an hour before the proper time. That's Christmas.'

He who made this speech was a young man about twenty-three years old, and the other personage in the dialogue was a young lady, who might be, perhaps, three years his junior. The 'papa' to whom the lady had alluded was the Rev. John Lownd, parson of Kirkby Cliffe, in Craven, and the scene was the parsonage library, as pleasant a little room as you would wish to see, in which the young man who thought Christmas to be a bore was at present sitting over the fire, in the parson's arm chair, with a novel in his hand, which he had been reading till he was interrupted by the parson's daughter. It was nearly time for him to dress for dinner, and the young lady was already dressed. She had entered the room on the pretext of looking for some book or paper, but perhaps her main object may have been to ask for some assistance from Maurice Archer in the work of decorating the parish church. The necessary ivy and holly branches had been collected, and the work was to be performed on the morrow. The day following would be Christmas Day. It must be acknowledged, that Mr Archer had not accepted the proposition made to him very graciously.

Maurice Archer was a young man as to whose future career in life many of his elder friends shook their heads and expressed much fear. It was not that his conduct was dangerously bad, or that he spent his money too fast, but that he was abominably conceited, so said these elder friends; and then there was the unfortunate fact of his being altogether beyond control. He had neither father, nor mother, nor uncle, nor guardian. He was the owner of a small property not far from Kirkby Cliffe, which gave him an income of some six or seven hundred a year, and he had altogether declined any of the professions which had been suggested to him. He had, in the course of the year now coming to a close, taken his degree at Oxford, with some academical honours, which were not high enough to confer distinction, and had already positively refused to be ordained, although, would he do so, a small living would be at his disposal on the death of a septuagenarian cousin. He intended, he said, to farm a portion of his own land, and had already begun to make amicable arrangements for buying up the interest of one of his two tenants. The rector of Kirkby Cliffe, the Rev. John Lownd, had been among his father's dearest friends, and he was now the parson's guest for the Christmas.

There had been many doubts in the parsonage before the young man had been invited. Mrs Lownd had considered that the visit would be dangerous. Their family consisted of two daughters, the youngest of whom was still a child; but Isabel was turned twenty, and if a young man were brought into the house, would it not follow, as a matter of course, that she should fall in love with him? That was the mother's first argument. 'Young people don't always fall in love,' said the father. 'But people will say that he is brought here on purpose,' said the mother, using her second argument. The parson, who in family matters generally had his own way, expressed an opinion that if they were to be governed by what other people might choose to say, their course of action would be very limited indeed. As for his girl, he did not think she would ever give her heart to any man before it had been asked; and as for the young man, – whose father had been for over thirty years his dearest friend, – if he chose to fall in love, he must run his chance, like other young men. Mr Lownd declared he knew nothing against him, except that he was, perhaps, a little self-willed; and so Maurice Archer came to Kirkby Cliffe, intending to spend two months in the same house with Isabel Lownd.

Hitherto, as far as the parents or the neighbours saw, and in their endeavours to see, the neighbours were very diligent, – there had been no love-making. Between Mabel, the young daughter, and Maurice, there had grown up a violent friendship, – so much so, that Mabel, who was fourteen, declared that Maurice Archer was 'the jolliest person' in the world. She called him Maurice, as did Mr and Mrs Lownd; and to Maurice, of course, she was Mabel. But between Isabel and Maurice it was always Miss Lownd and Mr Archer, as was proper. It was so, at least, with this difference, that each of them had got into a way of dropping, when possible, the other's name.

It was acknowledged throughout Craven, – which my readers of course know to be a district in the northern portion of the West Riding of Yorkshire, of which Skipton is the capital, – that Isabel Lownd was a very pretty girl. There were those who thought that Mary Manniwick, of Barden, excelled her; and others, again, expressed a preference for Fanny Grange, the pink-cheeked daughter of the surgeon at Giggleswick. No attempt shall here be made to award the palm of superior merit; but it shall be asserted boldly, that no man need desire a prettier girl with whom to fall in love than was Isabel Lownd. She was tall, active, fair, the very picture of feminine health, with bright gray eyes, a perfectly beautiful nose, – as is common to almost all girls belonging to Craven, – a mouth by no means delicately small, but eager, eloquent, and full of spirit, a well-formed short chin, with a dimple, and light brown hair, which was worn plainly smoothed over her brows, and fell in short curls behind her head. Of Maurice Archer it cannot be said that he was handsome. He had a snub nose; and a man so visaged can hardly be good-looking, though a girl with a snub nose may be very pretty. But he was a well-made young fellow, having a look of power about him, with dark-brown hair, cut very short, close shorn, with clear but rather small blue eyes, and an expression of countenance which allowed no one for a moment to think that he was weak in character, or a fool. His own place, called Hundlewick Hall, was about five miles from the parsonage. He had been there four or five times a week since his arrival at Kirkby Cliffe, and had already made arrangements for his own entrance upon the land in the following September. If a marriage were to come of it, the arrangement would be one very comfortable for the father and mother at Kirkby Cliffe. Mrs Lownd had already admitted as much as that to herself, though she still trembled for her girl. Girls are so prone to lose their hearts, whereas the young men of these

47

days are so very cautious and hard! That, at least, was Mrs Lownd's idea of girls and young men; and even at this present moment she was hardly happy about her child. Maurice, she was sure, had spoken never a word that might not have been proclaimed from the church tower; but her girl, she thought, was not quite the same as she had been before the young man had come among them. She was somewhat less easy in her manner, more preoccupied, and seemed to labour under a conviction that the presence in the house of Maurice Archer must alter the nature of her life. Of course it had altered the nature of her life, and of course she thought a great deal of Maurice Archer.

It had been chiefly at Mabel's instigation that Isabel had invited the co-operation of her father's visitor in the adornment of the church for Christmas Day. Isabel had expressed her opinion that Mr Archer didn't care a bit about such things, but Mabel declared that she had already extracted a promise from him. 'He'll do anything I ask him,' said Mabel, proudly. Isabel, however, had not cared to undertake the work in such company, simply under her sister's management, and had proffered the request herself. Maurice had not declined the task, – had indeed promised his assistance in some indifferent fashion, – but had accompanied his promise by a suggestion that Christmas was a bore! Isabel had rebuked him, and then he had explained. But his explanation, in Isabel's view of the case, only made the matter worse. Christmas to her was a very great affair indeed, – a festival to which the roast beef and the plum pudding were, no doubt, very necessary; but not by any means the essence, as he had chosen to consider them. Christmas a bore! No; a man who thought Christmas to be a bore should never be more to her than a mere acquaintance. She listened to his explanation, and then left the room, almost indignantly. Maurice, when she was gone, looked after her, and then read a page of his novel; but he was thinking of Isabel, and not of the book.

It was quite true that he had never said a word to her that might not have been declared from the church tower; but, nevertheless, he had thought about her a good deal. Those were days on which he was sure that he was in love with her, and would make her his wife. Then there came days on which he ridiculed himself for the idea. And now and then there was a day on which he asked himself whether he was sure that she would take him were he to ask her. There was sometimes an air with her, some little trick of the body, a manner of carrying her head when in his presence, which he was not physiognomist enough to investigate, but which in some way suggested doubts to him. It was on such occasions as this that he was most in love with her; and now she had left the room with that particular motion of her head which seemed almost to betoken contempt.

'If you mean to do anything before dinner you'd better do it at once,' said the parson, opening the door. Maurice jumped up, and in ten minutes was dressed and down in the dining-room. Isabel was there, but did not greet him. 'You'll come and help us to-morrow,' said Mabel, taking him by the arm and whispering to him.

'Of course I will,' said Maurice.

'And you won't go to Hundlewick again till after Christmas?'

'It won't take up the whole day to put up the holly.'

'Yes it will, – to do it nicely, – and nobody ever does any work the day before Christmas.'

'Except the cook,' suggested Maurice. Isabel, who heard the words, assumed that look of which he was already afraid, but said not a word. Then dinner was announced, and he gave his arm to the parson's wife.

Not a word was said about Christmas that evening. Isabel had threatened the young man with her father's displeasure on account of his expressed opinion as to the festival being a bore, but Mr Lownd was not himself one who talked a great deal about any Church festival. Indeed, it may be doubted whether his more enthusiastic daughter did not in her heart think him almost too indifferent on the subject. In the decorations of the church he, being an elderly man, and one with other duties to perform, would of course take no part. When the day came he would preach, no doubt, an appropriate sermon, would then eat his own roast beef and pudding with his ordinary appetite, would afterwards, if allowed to do so, sink into his arm-chair behind his book, – and then, for him, Christmas would be over. In all this there was no disrespect for the day, but it was hardly an enthusiastic observance. Isabel desired to greet the morning of her Saviour's birth with some special demonstration of joy. Perhaps from year to year she was somewhat disappointed, – but never before had it been hinted to her that Christmas was a bore.

On the following morning the work was to be commenced immediately after breakfast. The same thing had been done so often at Kirkby Cliffe, that the rector was quite used to it. David Drum, the clerk, who was also schoolmaster, and Barry Crossgrain, the parsonage gardener, would devote their services to the work in hand throughout the whole day, under the direction of Isabel. Mabel would of course be there assisting, as would also two daughters of a neighbouring farmer. Mrs Lownd would go down to the church about eleven, and stay till one, when the whole party would come up to the parsonage for refreshment. Mrs Lownd would not return to the work, but the others would remain there till it was finished, which finishing was never accomplished till candles had been burned in the church for a couple of hours. Then there would be more refreshments; but on this special day the parsonage dinner was never comfortable and orderly. The rector bore it all with good humour, but no one could say that he was enthusiastic in the matter. Mabel, who delighted in going up ladders, and leaning over the pulpit, and finding herself in all those odd parts of the church to which her imagination would stray during her father's sermons, but which were ordinarily inaccessible to her, took great delight in the work. And perhaps Isabel's delight had commenced with similar feelings. Immediately after breakfast, which was much hurried on the occasion, she put on her hat and hurried down to the church, without a word to Maurice on the subject. There was another whisper from Mabel, which was answered also with a whisper, and then Mabel also went. Maurice took up his novel, and seated himself comfortably by the parlour fire.

But again he did not read a word. Why had Isabel made herself so disagreeable, and why had she perked up her head as she left the room in that self-sufficient way, as though she was determined to show him that she did not want his assistance? Of course, she had understood well enough that he had not intended to say that the ceremonial observance of the day was a bore. He had spoken of the beef and the pudding, and she had chosen to pretend to misunderstand him. He would not go near the church. And as for his love, and his half-formed resolution to make her his wife, he would get over it altogether. If there were one thing more fixed with him than another, it was that on no consideration would he marry a girl who should give herself airs. Among them they might decorate the church as they pleased, and when he should see their handywork, – as he would do, of course, during the services of Christmas Day, – he would pass it by without a remark. So resolving, he again turned over a page or two of his novel, and then remembered that he was bound, at any rate, to keep his promise to his friend Mabel. Assuring himself that it was on that plea that he went, and on no other, he sauntered down to the church.

Kirkby Cliffe Church stands close upon the River Wharfe, about a quarter of a mile from the parsonage, which is on a steep hill-side running down from the moors to the stream. A prettier little church or graveyard you shall hardly find in England. Here, no large influx of population has necessitated the removal of the last home of the parishioners from beneath the shelter of the parish church. Every inhabitant of Kirkby Cliffe has, when dead, the privilege of rest among those green hillocks. Within the building is still room for tablets commemorative of the rectors and their wives and families, for there are none others in the parish to whom such honour is accorded. Without the walls, here and there, stand the tombstones of the farmers; while the undistinguished graves of the peasants lie about in clusters which, solemn though they be, are still picturesque. The church itself is old, and may probably be doomed before long to that kind of destruction which is called restoration; but hitherto it has been allowed to stand beneath all its weight of ivy, and has known but little change during the last two hundred years. Its old oak pews, and ancient exalted reading-desk and pulpit are offensive to many who come to see the spot; but Isabel Lownd is of opinion that neither the one nor the other could be touched, in the way of change, without profanation.

In the very porch Maurice Archer met Mabel, with her arms full of ivy branches, attended by David Drum. 'So you have come at last, Master Maurice?' she said.

'Come at last! Is that all the thanks I get? Now let me see what it is you're going to do. Is your sister here?'

'Of course she is. Barry is up in the pulpit, sticking holly branches round the sounding-board, and she is with him.'

'T' boorde's that rotten an' maaky, it'll be doon on Miss Is'bel's heede, an' Barty Crossgrain ain't more than or'nary

52

saft-handed,' said the clerk.

They entered the church, and there it was, just as Mabel had said. The old gardener was standing on the rail of the pulpit, and Isabel was beneath, handing up to him nails and boughs, and giving him directions as to their disposal. 'Naa, miss, naa; it wonot do that a-way,' said Barty. 'Thou'll ha' me o'er on to t'stances – thou wilt, that a-gait. Lard-a-mussy, miss, thou munnot clim' up, or thou'lt be doon, and brek thee banes, thee ull!' So saying, Barty Crossgrain, who had contented himself with remonstrating when called upon by his young mistress to imperil his own neck, jumped on to the floor of the pulpit and took hold of the young lady by both her ankles. As he did so, he looked up at her with anxious eyes, and steadied himself on his own feet, as though it might become necessary for him to perform some great feat of activity. All this Maurice Archer saw, and Isabel saw that he saw it. She was not well pleased at knowing that he should see her in that position, held by the legs by the old gardener, and from which she could only extricate herself by putting her hand on the old man's neck as she jumped down from her perch. But she did jump down, and then began to scold Crossgrain, as though the awkwardness had come from fault of his.

'I've come to help, in spite of the hard words you said to me yesterday, Miss Lownd,' said Maurice, standing on the lower steps of the pulpit. 'Couldn't I get up and do the things at the top?' But Isabel thought that Mr Archer could not get up and 'do the things at the top.' The wood was so far decayed that they must abandon the idea of ornamenting the sounding-board, and so both Crossgrain and Isabel descended into the body of the church.

Things did not go comfortably with them for the next hour. Isabel had certainly invited his co-operation, and therefore could not tell him to go away; and yet, such was her present feeling towards him, she could not employ him profitably, and with ease to herself. She was somewhat angry with him, and more angry with herself. It was not only that she had spoken hard words to him, as he had accused her of doing, but that, after the speaking of the hard words, she had been distant and cold in her manner to him. And yet he was so much to her! she liked him so well! – and though she had never dreamed of admitting to herself that she was in love with him, yet – yet it would be so pleasant to have the opportunity of asking herself whether she could not love him, should he ever give her a fair and open opportunity of searching her own heart on the matter. There had now sprung up some half-quarrel between them, and it was impossible that it could be set aside by any action on her part. She could not be otherwise than cold and haughty in her demeanour to him. Any attempt at reconciliation must come from him, and the longer that she continued to be cold and haughty, the less chance there was that it would come. And yet she knew that she had been right to rebuke him for what he had said. 'Christmas a bore!' She would rather lose his friendship for ever than hear such words from his mouth, without letting him know what she thought of them. Now he was there with her, and his coming could not but be taken as a sign of repentance. Yet she could not soften her manners to him, and become intimate with him, and playful, as had been her wont. He was allowed to pull about the masses of ivy, and to stick up branches of holly here and there at discretion; but what he did was done under Mabel's direction, and not under hers, – with the aid of one of the farmer's daughters, and not with her aid. In silence she continued to work round the chancel and communion-table, with Crossgrain, while Archer, Mabel, and David Drum used their taste and diligence in the nave and aisles of the little church. Then Mrs Lownd came among them, and things went more easily; but hardly a word had been spoken between Isabel and Maurice when, after sundry hints from David Drum as to the lateness of the hour, they left the church and went up to the parsonage for their luncheon.

Isabel stoutly walked on first, as though determined to show that she had no other idea in her head but that of reaching the parsonage as quickly as possible. Perhaps Maurice Archer had the same idea, for he followed her. Then he soon found that he was so far in advance of Mrs Lownd and the old gardener as to be sure of three minutes' uninterrupted conversation; for Mabel remained with her mother, making earnest supplication as to the expenditure of certain yards of green silk tape, which she declared to be necessary for the due performance of the work which they had in hand. 'Miss Lownd,' said Maurice, 'I think you are a little hard upon me.'

'In what way, Mr Archer?'

'You asked me to come down to the church, and you haven't spoken to me all the time I was there.'

'I asked you to come and work, not to talk,' she said.

'You asked me to come and work with you.'

'I don't think that I said any such thing; and you came at Mabel's request, and not at mine. When I asked you, you told me it was all – a bore. Indeed you said much worse than that. I certainly did not, mean to ask you again. Mabel asked you, and you came to oblige her. She talked to you, for I heard her; and I was half disposed to tell her not to laugh so much, and to remember that she was in church.'

'I did not laugh, Miss Lownd.'

'I was not listening especially to you.'

'Confess, now,' he said after a pause; 'don't you know that you misinterpreted me yesterday, and that you took what I said in a different spirit from my own.'

'No; I do not know it.'

'But you did. I was speaking of the holiday part of Christmas, which consists of pudding and beef, and is

55

surely subject to ridicule, if one chooses to ridicule pudding and beef. You answered me as though I had spoken slightingly of the religious feeling which belongs to the day.'

'You said that the whole thing was –; I won't repeat the word. Why should pudding and beef be a bore to you, when it is prepared as a sign that there shall be plenty on that day for people who perhaps don't have plenty on any other day of the year? The meaning of it is, that you don't like it all, because that which gives unusual enjoyment to poor people, who very seldom have any pleasure, is tedious to you. I don't like you for feeling it to be tedious. There! that's the truth. I don't mean to be uncivil, but –'

'You are very uncivil.'

'What am I to say, when you come and ask me?'

'I do not well know how you could be more uncivil, Miss Lownd. Of course it is the commonest thing in the world, that one person should dislike another. It occurs every day, and people know it of each other. I can perceive very well that you dislike me, and I have no reason to be angry with you for disliking me. You have a right to dislike me, if your mind runs that way. But it is very unusual for one person to tell another so to his face, – and more unusual to say so to a guest.' Maurice Archer, as he said this, spoke with a degree of solemnity to which she was not at all accustomed, so that she became frightened at what she had said. And not only was she frightened, but very unhappy also. She did not quite know whether she had or had not told him plainly that she disliked him, but she was quite sure that she had not intended to do so. She had been determined to scold him, – to let him see that, however much of real friendship there might be between them, she would speak her mind plainly, if he offended her; but she certainly had not desired to give him cause for lasting wrath against her. 'However,' continued Maurice, 'perhaps the truth is best after all, though it is so very unusual to hear such truths spoken.'

'I didn't mean to be uncivil,' stammered Isabel.

'But you meant to be true?'

'I meant to say what I felt about Christmas Day.' Then she paused a moment. 'If I have offended you, I beg your pardon.'

He looked at her and saw that her eyes were full of tears, and his heart was at once softened towards her. Should he say a word to her, to let her know that there was, – or, at any rate, that henceforth there should be no offence? But it occurred to him that if he did so, that word would mean so much, and would lead perhaps to the saying of other words, which ought not to be shown without forethought. And now, too, they were within the parsonage gate, and there was no time for speaking. 'You will go down again after lunch?' he asked.

'I don't know; – not if I can help it. Here's Papa.' She had begged his pardon, – had humbled herself before him. And he had not said a word in acknowledgment of the grace she had done him. She almost thought that she did dislike him, – really dislike him. Of course he had known what she meant, and he had chosen to misunderstand her and to take her, as it were, at an advantage. In her difficulty she had abjectly apologized to him, and he had not even deigned to express himself as satisfied with what she had done. She had known him to be conceited and masterful; but that, she had thought, she could forgive, believing it to be the common way with men, – imagining, perhaps, that a man was only the more worthy of love on account of such fault; but now she found that he was ungenerous also, and deficient in that chivalry without which a man can hardly appear at advantage in a woman's eyes. She went on into the house, merely touching her father's arm, as she passed him, and hurried up to her own room. 'Is there anything wrong with Isabel?' asked Mr

Lownd.

'She has worked too hard, I think, and is tired,' said Maurice.

Within ten minutes they were all assembled in the dining-room, and Mabel was loud in her narrative of the doings of the morning. Barty Crossgrain and David Drum had both declared the sounding-board to be so old that it mustn't even be touched, and she was greatly afraid that it would tumble down some day and 'squash papa' in the pulpit. The rector ridiculed the idea of any such disaster; and then there came a full description of the morning's scene, and of Barry's fears lest Isabel should 'brek her banes.' 'His own wig was almost off,' said Mabel, 'and he gave Isabel such a lug by the leg that she very nearly had to jump into his arms.'

'I didn't do anything of the kind,' said Isabel.

'You had better leave the sounding-board alone,' said the parson.

'We have left it alone, papa,' said Isabel, with great dignity. 'There are some other things that can't be done this year.' For Isabel was becoming tired of her task, and would not have returned to the church at all could she have avoided it.

'What other things?' demanded Mabel, who was as enthusiastic as ever. 'We can finish all the rest. Why shouldn't we finish it? We are ever so much more forward than we were last year, when David and Barty went to dinner. We've finished the Granby-Moore pew, and we never used to get to that till after luncheon.' But Mabel on this occasion had all the enthusiasm to herself. The two farmer's daughters, who had been brought up to the parsonage as usual, never on such occasions uttered a word. Mrs Lownd had completed her part of the work; Maurice could not trust himself to speak on the subject; and Isabel was dumb. Luncheon, however, was soon over, and something must be done. The four girls of course returned to their labours, but Maurice did not go with them, nor did he make any excuse for not doing so.

'I shall walk over to Hundlewick before dinner,' he said, as soon as they were all moving. The rector suggested that he would hardly be back in time. 'Oh, yes; ten miles – two hours and a half; and I shall have two hours there besides. I must see what they are doing with our own church, and how they mean to keep Christmas there. I'm not quite sure that I shan't go over there again tomorrow.' Even Mabel felt that there was something wrong, and said not a word in opposition to this wicked desertion.

He did walk to Hundlewick and back again, and when at Hundlewick he visited the church, though the church was a mile beyond his own farm. And he added something to the store provided for the beef and pudding of those who lived upon his own land; but of this he said nothing on his return to Kirkby Cliffe. He walked his dozen miles, and saw what was being done about the place, and visited the cottages of some who knew him, and yet was back at the parsonage in time for dinner. And during his walk he turned many things over in his thoughts, and endeavoured to make up his mind on one or two points. Isabel had never looked so pretty as when she jumped down into the pulpit, unless it was when she was begging his pardon for her want of courtesy to him. And though she had been, as he described it to himself, 'rather down upon him,' in regard to what he had said of Christmas, did he not like her the better for having an opinion of her own? And then, as he had stood for a few minutes leaning on his own gate, and looking at his own house at Hundlewick, it had occurred to him that he could hardly live there without a companion. After that he had walked back again, and was dressed for dinner, and in the drawing-room before any one of the family.

With poor Isabel the afternoon had gone much less satisfactorily. She found that she almost hated her work, that she really had a headache, and that she could put no heart into what she was doing. She was cross to Mabel, and almost surly to David Drum and Barty Grosgrain. The two farmer's daughters were allowed to do almost what they pleased with the holly branches, – a state of things which was most unusual, – and then Isabel, on her return to the parsonage, declared her intention of going to bed! Mrs Lownd, who had never before known her to do such a thing, was perfectly shocked. Go to bed, and not come down the whole of Christmas Eve! But Isabel was resolute. With a bad headache she would be better in bed than up. Were she to attempt to shake it off, she would be ill the next day. She did not want anything to eat, and would not take anything. No; she would not have any tea, but would go to bed at once. And to bed she went.

She was thoroughly discontented with herself, and felt that Maurice had, as it were, made up his mind against her forever. She hardly knew whether to be angry with herself or with him; but she did know very well that she had not intended really to quarrel with him. Of course she had been in earnest in what she had said; but he had taken her words as signifying so much more than she had intended! If he chose to quarrel with her, of course he must; but a friend could not, she was sure, care for her a great deal who would really be angry with her for such a trifle. Of course this friend did not care for her at all, – not the least, or he would not treat her so savagely. He had been quite savage to her, and she hated him for it. And yet she hated herself almost more. What right could she have had first to scold him, and then to tell him to his face that she disliked him? Of course he had gone away to Hundlewick. She would not have been a bit surprised if he had stayed there and never come back again. But he did come back, and she hated herself as she heard their voices as they all went in to dinner without her. It seemed to her that his voice was more cheery than ever. Last night and all the morning he had been silent and almost sullen, but now, the moment that she was away, he could talk and be full of spirits. She heard Mabel's ringing laughter downstairs, and she almost hated Mabel. It seemed to her that everybody was gay and happy because she was upstairs in her bed, and ill. Then there came a peal of laughter. She was glad that she was upstairs in bed, and ill. Nobody would have laughed, nobody would have been gay, had she been there. Maurice Archer liked them all, except her, – she was sure of that. And what could be more natural after her conduct to him? She had taken upon herself to lecture him, and of course he had not chosen to endure it. But of one thing she was quite sure, as she lay there, wretched in her solitude, – that now she would never alter her demeanour to him. He had chosen to be cold to her, and she would be like frozen ice to him. Again and again she heard their voices, and then, sobbing on her pillow, she fell asleep.

Showing How Isabel Lownd Told a Lie

On the following morning, – Christmas morning, – when she woke, her headache was gone, and she was able, as she dressed, to make some stern resolutions. The ecstasy of her sorrow was over, and she could see how foolish she had been to grieve as she had grieved. After all, what had she lost, or what harm had she done? She had never fancied that the young man was her lover, and she had never wished, – so she now told herself, – that he should become her lover. If one thing was plainer to her than another, it was this – that they two were not fitted for each other. She had sometimes whispered to herself, that if she were to marry at all, she would fain marry a clergyman. Now, no man could be more unlike a clergyman than Maurice Archer. He was, she thought, irreverent, and at no pains to keep his want of reverence out of sight, even in that house. He had said that Christmas was a bore, which, to her thinking, was abominable. Was she so poor a creature as to go to bed and cry for a man who had given her no sign that he even liked her, and of whose ways she disapproved so greatly, that even were he to offer her his hand she would certainly refuse it? She consoled herself for the folly of the preceding evening by assuring herself that she had really worked in the church till she was ill, and that she would have gone to bed, and must have gone to bed, had Maurice Archer never been seen or heard of at the parsonage. Other people went to bed when they had headaches, and why should not she? Then she resolved, as she dressed, that there should be no signs of illness, nor bit of ill-humour on her, on this sacred day. She would appear among them all full of mirth and happiness, and would laugh at the attack brought upon her by Barty Grosgrain's sudden fear in the pulpit; and she would greet Maurice Archer with all possible cordiality, wishing him a merry Christmas as she gave him her hand, and would make him understand in a moment that she had altogether forgotten their mutual bickerings. He should understand that, or should, at least, understand that she willed that it should all be regarded as forgotten. What was he to her, that any thought of him should be allowed to perplex her mind on such a day as this?

She went downstairs, knowing that she was the first up in the house, – the first, excepting the servants. She went into Mabel's room, and kissing her sister, who was only half awake, wished her many, many, many happy Christmases.

'Oh, Bell,' said Mabel, 'I do so hope you are better!'

'Of course I am better. Of course I am well. There is nothing for a headache like having twelve hours round of sleep. I don't know what made me so tired and so bad.'

'I thought it was something Maurice said,' suggested Mabel.

'Oh, dear, no. I think Barty had more to do with it than Mr Archer. The old fellow frightened me so when he made me think I was falling down. But get up, dear. Papa is in his room, and he'll be ready for prayers before you.'

Then she descended to the kitchen, and offered her good wishes to all the servants. To Barty, who always breakfasted there on Christmas mornings, she was especially kind, and said something civil about his work in the church.

'She'll 'bout brek her little heart for t''young mon there, an' he's naa true t' her,' said Barty, as soon as Miss Lownd had closed the kitchen door; showing, perhaps, that he knew more of the matter concerning herself than she did.

She then went into the parlour to prepare the breakfast, and to put a little present, which she had made for her father, on his plate; – when, whom should she see but Maurice Archer!

It was a fact known to all the household, and a fact that had not recommended him at all to Isabel, that Maurice never did come downstairs in time for morning prayers. He was always the last; and, though in most respects a very active man, seemed to be almost a sluggard in regard to lying in bed late. As far as she could remember at the moment, he had never been present at prayers a single morning since the first after his arrival at the parsonage, when shame, and a natural feeling of strangeness in the house, had brought him out of his bed. Now he was there half an hour before the appointed time, and during that half-hour she was doomed to be alone with him. But her courage did not for a moment desert her.

'This is a wonder!' she said, as she took his hand. 'You will have a long Christmas Day, but I sincerely hope that it may be a happy one.'

'That depends on you,' said he.

'I'll do everything I can,' she answered. 'You shall only have a very little bit of roast beef, and the unfortunate

63

pudding shan't be brought near you.' Then she looked in his face, and saw that his manner was very serious, – almost solemn, – and quite unlike his usual ways. 'Is anything wrong?' she asked.

'I don't know; I hope not. There are things which one has to say which seem to be so very difficult when the time comes. Miss Lownd, I want you to love me.'

'What!' She started back as she made the exclamation, as though some terrible proposition had wounded her ears. If she had ever dreamed of his asking for her love, she had dreamed of it as a thing that future days might possibly produce; – when he should be altogether settled at Hundlewick, and when they should have got to know each other intimately by the association of years.

'Yes, I want you to love me, and to be my wife. I don't know how to tell you; but I love you better than anything and everything in the world, – better than all the world put together. I have done so from the first moment that I saw you; I have. I knew how it would be the very first instant I saw your dear face, and every word you have spoken, and every look out of your eyes, has made me love you more and more. If I offended you yesterday, I will beg your pardon.'

'Oh, no,' she said.

'I wish I had bitten my tongue out before I had said what I did about Christmas Day. I do, indeed. I only meant, in a half-joking way, to – to – to. But I ought to have known you wouldn't like it, and I beg your pardon. Tell me, Isabel, do you think that you can love me?'

Not half an hour since she had made up her mind that, even were he to propose to her, – which she then knew to be absolutely impossible, – she would certainly refuse him. He was not the sort of man for whom she would be a fitting wife; and she had made up her mind also, at the same time, that she did not at all care for him, and that he certainly did not in the least care for her. And now the offer had absolutely been made to her! Then came across her mind an idea that he ought in the first place to have gone to her father; but as to that she was not quite sure. Be that as it might, there he was, and she must give him some answer. As for thinking about it, that was altogether beyond her. The shock to her was too great to allow of her thinking. After some fashion, which afterwards was quite unintelligible to herself, it seemed to her, at that moment, that duty, and maidenly reserve, and filial obedience, all required her to reject him instantly. Indeed, to have accepted him would have been quite beyond her power. 'Dear Isabel,' said he, 'may I hope that some day you will love me?'

'Oh, Mr Archer, don't,' she said. 'Do not ask me.'

'Why should I not ask you?'

'It can never be.' This she said quite plainly, and in a voice that seemed to him to settle his fate forever; and yet at the moment her heart was full of love towards him. Though she could not think, she could feel. Of course she loved him. At the very moment in which she was telling him that it could never be, she was elated by an almost ecstatic triumph, as she remembered all her fears, and now knew that the man was at her feet.

When a girl first receives the homage of a man's love, and receives it from one whom, whether she loves him or not, she thoroughly respects, her earliest feeling is one of victory, – such a feeling as warmed the heart of a conqueror in the Olympian games. He is the spoil of her spear, the fruit of her prowess, the quarry brought down by her own bow and arrow. She, too, by some power of her own which she is hitherto quite unable to analyze, has stricken a man to the very heart, so as to compel him for the moment to follow wherever she may lead him. So it was with Isabel Lownd as she stood there, conscious of the eager gaze which was fixed upon her face, and fully alive to the anxious tones of her lover's voice. And yet she could only deny him. Afterwards, when she thought of it, she could not imagine why it had been so with her; but, in spite of her great love, she continued to tell herself that there was some obstacle which could never be overcome, – or was it that a certain maidenly reserve sat so strong within her bosom that she could not bring herself to own to him that he was dear to her?

'Never!' exclaimed Maurice, despondently.

'Oh, no!'

'But why not? I will be very frank with you, dear. I did think you liked me a little before that affair in the study.' Like him a little! Oh, how she had loved him! She knew it now, and yet not for worlds could she tell him so. 'You are not still angry with me, Isabel?'

'No; not angry.'

'Why should you say never? Dear Isabel, cannot you try to love me?' Then he attempted to take her hand, but she recoiled at once from his touch, and did feel something of anger against him in that he should thus refuse to take her word. She knew not what it was that she desired of him, but certainly he should not attempt to take her hand, when she told him plainly that she could not love him. A red spot rose to each of her cheeks as again he pressed her. 'Do you really mean that you can never, never love me?' She muttered some answer, she knew not what, and then he turned from her, and stood looking out upon the snow which had fallen during the night. She kept her ground for a few seconds, and then escaped through the door, and up to her own bedroom. When once there, she burst out into tears. Could it be possible that she had thrown away forever her own happiness, because she had been too silly to give a true answer to an honest question? And was this the enjoyment and content which she had promised herself for Christmas Day? But surely, surely he would come to her again. If he really loved her as he had declared, if it was true that ever since his arrival at Kirkby

Cliffe he had thought of her as his wife, he would not abandon her because in the first tumult of her surprise she had lacked courage to own to him the truth; and then in the midst of her tears there came upon her that delicious recognition of a triumph which, whatever be the victory won, causes such elation to the heart! Nothing, at any rate, could rob her of this – that he had loved her. Then, as a thought suddenly struck her, she ran quickly across the passage, and in a moment was upstairs, telling her tale with her mother's arm close folded round her waist.

In the meantime Mr Lownd had gone down to the parlour, and had found Maurice still looking out upon the snow. He, too, with some gentle sarcasm, had congratulated the young man on his early rising, as he expressed the ordinary wish of the day. 'Yes,' said Maurice, 'I had something special to do. Many happy Christmases, sir! I don't know much about its being happy to me.'

'Why, what ails you?'

'It's a nasty sort of day, isn't it?' said Maurice.

'Does that trouble you? I rather like a little snow on Christmas Day. It has a pleasant, old-fashioned look. And there isn't enough to keep even an old woman at home.'

'I dare say not,' said Maurice, who was still beating about the bush, having something to tell, but not knowing how to tell it. 'Mr Lownd, I should have come to you first, if it hadn't been for an accident.'

'Come to me first! What accident?'

'Yes; only I found Miss Lownd down here this morning, and I asked her to be my wife. You needn't be unhappy about it, sir. She refused me point blank.'

'You must have startled her, Maurice. You have startled me, at any rate.'

'There was nothing of that sort, Mr Lownd. She took it all very easily. I think she does take things easily.' Poor Isabel! 'She just told me plainly that it never could be so, and then she walked out of the room.'

'I don't think she expected it, Maurice.'

'Oh, dear no! I'm quite sure she didn't. She hadn't thought about me any more than if I were an old dog. I suppose men do make fools of themselves sometimes. I shall get over it, sir.'

'Oh, I hope so.'

'I shall give up the idea of living here. I couldn't do that. I shall probably sell the property, and go to Africa.'

'Go to Africa!'

'Well, yes. It's as good a place as any other, I suppose. It's wild, and a long way off, and all that kind of thing. As this is Christmas, I had better stay here to-day, I suppose.'

'Of course you will.'

'If you don't mind, I'll be off early to-morrow, sir. It's a kind of thing, you know, that does flurry a man. And then my being here may be disagreeable to her; – not that I suppose she thinks about me any more than if I were an old cow.'

It need hardly be remarked that the rector was a much older man than Maurice Archer, and that he therefore knew the world much better. Nor was he in love. And he had, moreover, the advantage of a much closer knowledge of the young lady's character than could be possessed by the lover. And, as it happened, during the last week, he had been fretted by fears expressed by his wife, – fears which were altogether opposed to Archer's present despondency and African resolutions. Mrs Lownd had been uneasy, – almost more than uneasy, – lest poor dear Isabel should be stricken at her heart; whereas, in regard to that young man, she didn't believe that he cared a bit for her girl. He ought not to have been brought into the house. But he was there, and what could they do? The rector was of the opinion that things would come straight, – that they would be straightened not by any lover's propensities on the part of his guest, as to which he protested himself to be altogether indifferent, but by his girl's good sense. His Isabel would never allow herself to be seriously affected by a regard for a young man who had made no overtures to her. That was the rector's argument; and perhaps, within his own mind, it was backed by a feeling that, were she so weak, she must stand the consequence. To him it seemed to be an absurd degree of caution that two young people should not be brought together in the same house lest one should fall in love with the other. And he had seen no symptoms of such love. Nevertheless his wife had fretted him, and he had been uneasy. Now the shoe was altogether on the other foot. The young man was the despondent lover, and was asserting that he must go instantly to Africa, because the young lady treated him like an old dog, and thought no more about him than of an old cow.

A father in such a position can hardly venture to hold out hopes to a lover, even though he may approve of the man as a suitor for his daughter's hand. He cannot answer for his girl, nor can he very well urge upon a lover the expediency of renewing his suit. In this case Mr Lownd did think, that in spite of the cruel, determined obduracy which his daughter was said to have displayed, she might probably be softened by constancy and perseverance. But he knew nothing of the circumstances, and could only suggest that Maurice should not take his place for the first stage on his way to Africa quite at once. 'I do not think you need hurry away because of Isabel,' he said, with a gentle smile.

'I couldnt stand it, – I couldn't indeed,' said Maurice, impetuously. 'I hope I didn't do wrong in speaking to her when I found her here this morning. If you had come first I should have told you.'

I could only have referred you to her, my dear boy. Come – here they are; and now we will have prayers.' As he spoke, Mrs Lownd entered the room, followed closely by Mabel, and then at a little distance by Isabel. The three maid-servants were standing behind in a line, ready to come in for prayers. Maurice could not but feel that Mrs Lownd's manner to him was especially affectionate; for, in truth, hitherto she had kept somewhat aloof from him, as though he had been a ravening wolf. Now she held him by the hand, and had a spark of motherly affection in her eyes, as she, too, repeated her Christmas greeting. It might well be so, thought Maurice. Of course she would be more kind to him than ordinary, if she knew that he was a poor blighted individual. It was a thing of course that Isabel should have told her mother, equally a thing of course that he should be pitied and treated tenderly. But on the next day he would be off. Such tenderness as that would kill him.

As they sat at breakfast, they all tried to be very gracious to each other. Mabel was sharp enough to know that something special had happened, but could not quite be sure what it was. Isabel struggled very hard to make little speeches about the day, but cannot be said to have succeeded well. Her mother, who had known at once how it was with her child, and had required no positive answers to direct questions to enable her to assume that Isabel was now devoted to her lover, had told her girl that if the man's love were worth having, he would surely ask her again. 'I don't think he will, mamma,' Isabel had whispered, with her face half-hidden on her mother's arm. 'He must be very unlike other men if he does not,' Mrs Lownd had said, resolving that the opportunity should not be wanting. Now she was very gracious to Maurice, speaking before him as though he were quite one of the family. Her trembling maternal heart had feared him, while she thought that he might be a ravening wolf, who would steal away her daughter's heart, leaving nothing in return; but now that he had proved himself willing to enter the fold as a useful domestic sheep, nothing could be too good for him. The parson himself, seeing all this,

70

understanding every turn in his wife's mind, and painfully anxious that no word might be spoken which should seem to entrap his guest, strove diligently to talk as though nothing was amiss. He spoke of his sermon, and of David Drum, and of the allowance of pudding that was to be given to the inmates of the neighbouring poor-house. There had been a subscription, so as to relieve the rates from the burden of the plum-pudding, and Mr Lownd thought that the farmers had not been sufficiently liberal. 'There's Furness, at Loversloup, gave us half-a-crown. I told him he ought to be ashamed of himself. He declared to me to my face that if he could find puddings for his own bairns, that was enough for him.'

'The richest farmer in these parts, Maurice,' said Mrs Lownd.

'He holds above three hundred acres of land, and could stock double as many, if he had them,' said the would-be indignant rector, who was thinking a great deal more of his daughter than of the poor-house festival. Maurice answered him with a word or two, but found it very hard to assume any interest in the question of the pudding. Isabel was more hard-hearted, he thought, than even Farmer Furness, of Loversloup. And why should he trouble himself about these people, – he, who intended to sell his acres, and go away to Africa? But he smiled and made some reply, and buttered his toast, and struggled hard to seem as though nothing ailed him.

The parson went down to church before his wife, and Mabel went with him. 'Is anything wrong with Maurice Archer?' she asked her father.

'Nothing, I hope,' said he.

'Because he doesn't seem to be able to talk this morning.'

'Everybody isn't a chatter-box like you, Mab.'

'I don't think I chatter more than mamma, or Bell. Do you know, papa, I think Bell has quarrelled with Maurice

Archer.'

'I hope not. I should be very sorry that there should be any quarrelling at all – particularly on this day. Well, I think you've done it very nicely; and it is none the worse because you've left the sounding-board alone.' Then Mabel went over to David Drum's cottage, and asked after the condition of Mrs Drum's plum-pudding.

No one had ventured to ask Maurice Archer whether he would stay in church for the sacrament, but he did. Let us hope that no undue motive of pleasing Isabel Lownd had any effect upon him at such a time. But it did please her. Let us hope also that, as she knelt beside her lover at the low railing, her young heart was not too full of her love. That she had been thinking of him throughout her father's sermon, – thinking of him, then resolving that she would think of him no more, and then thinking of him more than ever, – must be admitted. When her mother had told her that he would come again to her, she had not attempted to assert that, were he to do so, she would again reject him. Her mother knew all her secret, and, should he not come again, her mother would know that she was heart-broken. She had told him positively that she would never love him. She had so told him, knowing well that at the very moment he was dearer to her than all the world beside. Why had she been so wicked as to lie to him? And if now she were punished for her lie by his silence, would she not be served properly? Her mind ran much more on the subject of this great sin which she had committed on that very morning, – that sin against one who loved her so well, and who desired to do good to her, – than on those general arguments in favour of Christian kindness and forbearance which the preacher drew from the texts applicable to Christmas Day. All her father's eloquence was nothing to her. On ordinary occasions he had no more devoted listener; but, on this morning, she could only exercise her spirit by repenting her own unchristian conduct. And then he came and knelt beside her at that sacred moment! It was impossible that he should forgive her, because he could not know that she had sinned against him.

There were certain visits to her poorer friends in the immediate village which, according to custom, she would make after church. When Maurice and Mrs Lownd went up to the parsonage, she and Mabel made their usual round. They all welcomed her, but they felt that she was not quite herself with them, and even Mabel asked her what ailed her.

'Why should anything ail me? – only I don't like walking in the snow.'

Then Mabel took courage. 'If there is a secret, Bell, pray tell me. I would tell you any secret.'

'I don't know what you mean,' said Isabel, almost crossly.

'Is there a secret, Bell? I'm sure there is a secret about Maurice.'

'Don't, – don't,' said Isabel.

'I do like Maurice so much. Don't you like him?'

'Pray do not talk about him, Mabel.'

'I believe he is in love with you, Bell; and, if he is, I think you ought to be in love with him. I don't know how you could have anybody nicer. And he is going to live at Hundlewick, which would be such great fun. Would not papa like it?'

'I don't know. Oh, dear! – oh, dear!' Then she burst out into tears, and walking out of the village, told Mabel the whole truth. Mabel heard it with consternation, and expressed her opinion that, in these circumstances, Maurice would never ask again to make her his wife.

'Then I shall die,' said Isabel, frankly.

In spite of her piteous condition and near prospect of death, Isabel Lownd completed her round of visits among her old friends. That Christmas should be kept in some way by every inhabitant of Kirkby Cliffe, was a thing of course. The district is not poor, and plenty on that day was rarely wanting. But Parson Lownd was not what we call a rich man; and there was no resident squire in the parish. The farmers, comprehending well their own privileges, and aware that the obligation of gentle living did not lie on them, were inclined to be close-fisted; and thus there was sometimes a difficulty in providing for the old and the infirm. There was a certain ancient widow in the village, of the name of Mucklewort, who was troubled with three orphan grandchildren and a lame daughter; and Isabel had, some days since, expressed a fear up at the parsonage that the good things of this world might be scarce in the old widow's cottage. Something had, of course, been done for the old woman, but not enough, as Isabel had thought. 'My dear,' her mother had said, 'it is no use trying to make very poor people think that they are not poor.'

'It is only one day in the year,' Isabel had pleaded.

'What you give in excess to one, you take from another,' replied Mrs Lownd, with the stern wisdom which experience teaches. Poor Isabel could say nothing further, but had feared greatly that the rations in Mrs Mucklewort's abode would be deficient. She now entered the cottage, and found the whole family at that moment preparing themselves for the consumption of a great Christmas banquet. Mrs Mucklewort, whose temper was not always the best in the world, was radiant. The children were silent, open-eyed, expectant, and solemn. The lame aunt was in the act of transferring a large lump of beef, which seemed to be commingled in a most inartistic way with

74

potatoes and cabbage, out of a pot on to the family dish. At any rate there was plenty; for no five appetites – had the five all been masculine, adult, and yet youthful – could, by any feats of strength, have emptied that dish at a sitting. And Isabel knew well that there had been pudding. She herself had sent the pudding; but that, as she was well aware, had not been allowed to abide its fate till this late hour of the day. 'I'm glad you're all so well employed,' said Isabel. 'I thought you had done dinner long ago. I won't stop a minute now.'

The old woman got up from her chair, and nodded her head, and held out her withered old hand to be shaken. The children opened their mouths wider than ever, and hoped there might be no great delay. The lame aunt curtseyed and explained the circumstances. 'Beef, Miss Isabel, do take a mortal time t' boil; and it ain't no wise good for t' bairns to have it any ways raw.' To this opinion Isabel gave her full assent, and expressed her gratification that the amount of beef should be sufficient to require so much cooking. Then the truth came out. 'Muster Archer just sent us over from Rowdy's a meal's meat with a vengence; God bless him!' 'God bless him!' crooned out the old woman, and the children muttered some unintelligible sound, as though aware that duty required them to express some Amen to the prayer of their elders. Now Rowdy was the butcher living at Grassington, some six miles away, – for at Kirkby Cliffe there was no butcher. Isabel smiled all round upon them sweetly, with her eyes full of tears, and then left the cottage without a word.

He had done this because she had expressed a wish that these people should be kindly treated, – had done it without a syllable spoken to her or to any one, – had taken trouble, sending all the way to Grassington for Mrs Mucklewort's beef! No doubt he had given other people beef, and had whispered no word of his kindness to any one at the rectory. And yet she had taken upon herself to rebuke him, because he had not cared for Christmas Day! As she walked along, silent, holding Mabel's hand, it seemed to her that of all men he was the most perfect. She had rebuked him, and had then told him – with incredible falseness – that she did not like him; and after that, when he had proposed to her in the kindest, noblest manner, she had rejected him, – almost as though he had not been good enough for her! She felt now as though she would like to bite the tongue out of her head for such misbehavior.

'Was not that nice of him?' said Mabel. But Isabel could not answer the question. 'I always thought he was like that,' continued the younger sister. 'If he were my lover, I'd do anything he asked me, because he is so good-natured.'

'Don't talk to me,' said Isabel. And Mabel, who comprehended something of the condition of her sister's mind, did not say another word on their way back to the parsonage.

It was the rule of the house that on Christmas Day they should dine at four o'clock; – a rule which almost justified the very strong expression with which Maurice first offended the young lady whom he loved. To dine at one or two o'clock is a practice which has its recommend-ations. It suits the appetite, is healthy, and divides the day into two equal halves, so that no man so dining fancies that his dinner should bring to him an end of his usual occupations. And to dine at six, seven, or eight is well adapted to serve several purposes of life. It is convenient, as inducing that gentle lethargy which will sometimes follow the pleasant act of eating at a time when the work of the day is done; and it is both fashionable and comfortable. But to dine at four is almost worse than not to dine at all. The rule, however, existed at Kirkby Cliffe parsonage in regard to this one special day in the year, and was always obeyed.

On this occasion Isabel did not see her lover from the moment in which he left her at the church door till they met at table. She had been with her mother, but her mother had said not a word to her about Maurice. Isabel knew very well that they two had walked home together from the church, and she had thought that her best chance lay in the possibility that he would have spoken of what had occurred during the walk. Had this been so, surely her mother would have told her; but not a word had been said; and even with her mother Isabel had been too shamefaced to ask a question. In truth, Isabel's name had not been mentioned between them, nor had any allusion been made to what had taken place during the morning. Mrs Lownd had been too wise and too wary, – too well aware of what was really due to her daughter, – to bring up the subject herself; and he had been silent, subdued, and almost sullen. If he could not get an acknowledgment of affection from the girl herself, he certainly would not endeavour to extract a cold compliance by the mother's aid. Africa, and a disruption of all the plans of his life, would be better to him than that. But Mrs Lownd knew very well how it was with him; knew how it was with them both; and was aware that in such a condition things should be allowed to arrange themselves. At dinner, both she and the rector were full of mirth and good humour, and Mabel, with great glee, told the story of Mrs Muckelwort's dinner. 'I don't want to destroy your pleasure,' she said, bobbing her head at Maurice; 'but it did look so nasty! Beef should always be roast beef on Christmas Day.'

'I told the butcher it was to be roast beef,' said Maurice, sadly.

'I dare say the little Muckelworts would just as soon have it boiled,' said Mrs Lownd. 'Beef is beef to them, and a pot for boiling is an easy apparatus.'

'If you had beef, Miss Mab, only once or twice a year,'

said her father, 'you would not care whether it were roast or boiled.' But Isabel spoke not a word. She was most anxious to join the conversation about Mrs Mucklewort, and would have liked much to give testimony to the generosity displayed in regard to quantity; but she found that she could not do it. She was absolutely dumb. Maurice Archer did speak, making, every now and then, a terrible effort to be jocose; but Isabel from first to last was silent. Only by silence could she refrain from a renewed deluge of tears.

In the evening two or three girls came in with their younger brothers, the children of farmers of the better class in the neighbourhood, and the usual attempts were made at jollity. Games were set on foot, in which even the rector joined, instead of going to sleep behind his book, and Mabel, still conscious of her sister's wounds, did her very best to promote the sports. There was blindman's-buff, and hide and seek, and snapdragon, and forfeits, and a certain game with music and chairs, – very prejudicial to the chairs, – in which it was everybody's object to sit down as quickly as possible when the music stopped. In the game Isabel insisted on playing, because she could do that alone. But even to do this was too much for her. The sudden pause could hardly be made without a certain hilarity of spirit, and her spirits were unequal to any exertion. Maurice went through his work like a man, was blinded, did his forfeits, and jostled for the chairs with the greatest diligence; but in the midst of it all he, too, was as solemn as a judge, and never once spoke a single word to Isabel. Mrs Lownd, who usually was not herself much given to the playing of games, did on this occasion make an effort, and absolutely consented to cry the forfeits; but Mabel was wonderfully quiet, so that the farmer's daughters hardly perceived that there was anything amiss.

It came to pass, after a while, that Isabel had retreated to her room, – not for the night, as it was as yet hardly eight o'clock, – and she certainly would not disappear till the visitors had taken their departure, – a ceremony which was sure to take place with the greatest punctuality at ten, after an early supper. But she had escaped for a while, and in the meantime some frolic was going on which demanded the absence of one of the party from the room, in order that mysteries might be arranged of which the absent one should remain in ignorance. Maurice was thus banished, and desired to remain in desolation for the space of five minutes; but, just as he had taken up his position, Isabel descended with slow, solemn steps, and found him standing at her father's study door. She was passing on, and had almost entered the drawing-room, when he called her. 'Miss Lownd,' he said. Isabel stopped, but did not speak; she was absolutely beyond speaking. The excitement of the day had been so great, that she was all but overcome by it, and doubted, herself, whether she would be able to keep up appearances till the supper should be over, and she should be relieved for the night. 'Would you let me say one word to you?' said Maurice. She bowed her head and went with him into the study.

Five minutes had been allowed for the arrangement of the mysteries, and at the end of the five minutes Maurice was authorized, by the rules of the game, to return to the room. But he did not come, and upon Mabel's suggesting that possibly he might not be able to see his watch in the dark, she was sent to fetch him. She burst into the study, and there she found the truant and her sister, very close, standing together on the hearthrug. 'I didn't know you were here, Bell,' she exclaimed. Whereupon Maurice, as she declared afterwards, jumped round the table after her, and took her in his arms and kissed her. 'But you must come,' said Mabel, who accepted the embrace with perfect goodwill.

'Of course you must. Do go, pray, and I'll follow, – almost immediately.' Mabel perceived at once that her sister had altogether recovered her voice.

'I'll tell 'em you're coming,' said Mabel, vanishing.

'You must go now,' said Isabel. 'They'll all be away soon, and then you can talk about it.' As she spoke, he was standing with his arm round her waist, and Isabel Lownd was the happiest girl in all Craven.

Mrs Lownd knew all about it from the moment in which Maurice Archer's prolonged absence had become cause of complaint among the players. Her mind had been intent upon the matter, and she had become well aware that it was only necessary that the two young people should be alone together for a few moments. Mabel had entertained great hopes, thinking, however, that perhaps three or four years must be passed in melancholy gloomy doubts before the path of true love could be made to run smooth; but the light had shone upon her as soon as she saw them standing together. The parson knew nothing about it till the supper was over. Then, when the front door was open, and the farmer's daughters had been cautioned not to get themselves more wet than they could help in the falling snow, Maurice said a word to his future father-in-law. 'She has consented at last, sir. I hope you have nothing to say against it.'

'Not a word,' said the parson, grasping the young man's hand, and remembering as he did so, the extension of the time over which that phrase 'at last' was supposed to spread itself.

Maurice had been promised some further opportunity of 'talking about it,' and of course claimed a fulfillment of the promise. There was a difficulty about it, as Isabel, having now been assured of her happiness, was anxious to talk about it all to her mother rather than to him; but he was imperative, and there came at last for him a quarter of an hour of delicious triumph in that very spot on which he had been so scolded for saying that Christmas was a bore. 'You were so very sudden,' said Isabel, excusing herself for her conduct in the morning.

'But you did love me?'

'If I do now, that ought to be enough for you. But I did, and I've been so unhappy since; and I thought that, perhaps, you would never speak to me again. But it was all your fault; you were so sudden. And then you ought to have asked papa first, – you know you ought. But, Maurice, you will promise me one thing. You won't ever again say that Christmas Day is a bore!'

Christmas at Mellstock

From *Under the Greenwood Tree*

Thomas Hardy

Hardy published Under the Greenwood Tree *in 1872, though it's set around 1840. This extract from chapter 6 gives a vivid picture of a Christmas morning in Dorset in those days. It's substantially based on Hardy's own memories.*

They made preparations for going to church as usual; Dick with extreme alacrity, though he would not definitely consider why he was so religious. His wonderful nicety in brushing and cleaning his best light boots had features which elevated it to the rank of an art. Every particle and speck of last week's mud was scraped and brushed from toe and heel; new blacking from the packet was carefully mixed and made use of, regardless of expense. A coat was laid on and polished; then another coat for increased blackness; and lastly a third, to give the perfect and mirror-like jet which the hoped-for rencounter demanded.

It being Christmas-day, the tranter prepared himself with Sunday particularity. Loud sousing and snorting noises were heard to proceed from a tub in the back quarters of the dwelling, proclaiming that he was there performing his great Sunday wash, lasting half-an-hour, to which his washings on working-day mornings were mere flashes in the pan. Vanishing into the outhouse with a large brown towel, and the above-named bubblings and snortings being carried on for about twenty minutes, the tranter would appear round the edge of the door, smelling like a summer fog, and looking as if he had just narrowly escaped a watery grave with the loss of much of his clothes, having since been weeping bitterly till his eyes were red; a crystal drop of water hanging ornamentally at the bottom of each ear, one at the tip of his nose, and others in the form of spangles about his hair.

After a great deal of crunching upon the sanded stone floor by the feet of father, son, and grandson as they moved to and fro in these preparations, the bass-viol and fiddles were taken from their nook, and the strings examined and screwed a little above concert-pitch, that they might keep their tone when the service began, to obviate the awkward contingency of having to retune them at the back of the gallery during a cough, sneeze, or amen – an inconvenience which had been known to arise in damp wintry weather.

The three left the door and paced down Mellstock-lane and across the ewe-lease, bearing under their arms the instruments in faded green-baize bags, and old brown music-books in their hands; Dick continually finding himself in advance of the other two, and the tranter moving on with toes turned outwards to an enormous angle.

At the foot of an incline the church became visible through the north gate, or 'church hatch,' as it was called here. Seven agile figures in a clump were observable beyond, which proved to be the choristers waiting; sitting on an altar-tomb to pass the time, and letting their heels dangle against it. The musicians being now in sight, the youthful party scampered off and rattled up the old wooden stairs of the gallery like a regiment of cavalry; the other boys of the parish waiting outside and observing birds, cats, and other creatures till the vicar entered, when they suddenly subsided into sober church-goers, and passed down the aisle with echoing heels.

The gallery of Mellstock Church had a status and sentiment of its own. A stranger there was regarded with a feeling altogether differing from that of the congregation below towards him. Banished from the nave as an intruder whom no originality could make interesting, he was received above as a curiosity that no unfitness could render dull. The gallery, too, looked down upon and knew the habits of the nave to its remotest peculiarity, and had an extensive stock of exclusive information about it; whilst the nave knew nothing of the gallery folk, as gallery folk, beyond their loud-sounding minims and chest notes. Such topics as that the clerk was always chewing tobacco except at the moment of crying amen; that he had a dust-hole in his pew; that during the sermon certain young daughters of the village had left off caring to read anything so mild as the marriage service for some years, and now regularly studied the one which chronologically follows it; that a pair of lovers touched fingers through a knot-hole between their pews in the manner ordained by their great exemplars, Pyramus and Thisbe; that Mrs. Ledlow, the farmer's wife, counted her money and reckoned her week's marketing expenses during the first lesson – all news to those below – were stale subjects here.

Old William sat in the centre of the front row, his violoncello between his knees and two singers on each hand. Behind him, on the left, came the treble singers and Dick; and on the right the tranter and the tenors. Further back was old Mail with the altos and supernumeraries. ...

Ever afterwards the young man could recollect individually each part of the service of that bright Christmas morning, and the trifling occurrences which took place as its minutes slowly drew along; the duties of that day dividing themselves by a complete line from the services of other times. The tunes they that morning essayed remained with him for years, apart from all others; also the text; also the appearance of the layer of dust upon the capitals of the piers; that the holly-bough in the chancel archway was hung a little out of the centre – all the ideas, in short, that creep into the mind when reason is only exercising its lowest activity through the eye.

By chance or by fate, another young man who attended Mellstock Church on that Christmas morning had towards the end of the service the same instinctive perception of an interesting presence, in the shape of the same bright maiden, though his emotion reached a far less developed stage. And there was this difference, too, that the person in question was surprised at his condition, and sedulously endeavoured to reduce himself to his normal state of mind. He was the young vicar, Mr Maybold.

The music on Christmas mornings was frequently below the standard of church-performances at other times. The boys were sleepy from the heavy exertions of the night; the men were slightly wearied; and now, in addition to these constant reasons, there was a dampness in the atmosphere that still further aggravated the evil. Their strings, from the recent long exposure to the night air, rose whole semitones, and snapped with a loud twang at the most silent moment; which necessitated more retiring than ever to the back of the gallery, and made the gallery throats quite husky with the quantity of coughing and hemming required for tuning in. The vicar looked cross.

When the singing was in progress there was suddenly discovered to be a strong and shrill reinforcement from some point, ultimately found to be the school-girls' aisle. At every attempt it grew bolder and more distinct. At the third time of singing, these intrusive feminine voices were as mighty as those of the regular singers; in fact, the flood of sound from this quarter assumed such an individuality, that it had a time, a key, almost a tune of its own, surging upwards when the gallery plunged downwards, and the reverse.

Now this had never happened before within the memory of man. The girls, like the rest of the con-gregation, had always been humble and respectful followers of the gallery; singing at sixes and sevens if without gallery leaders; never interfering with the ordinances of these practised artists – having no will, union, power, or proclivity except it was given them from the established choir enthroned above them.

A good deal of desperation became noticeable in the gallery throats and strings, which continued throughout the musical portion of the service. Directly the fiddles were laid down, Mr Penny's spectacles put in their sheath, and the text had been given out, an indignant whispering began.

'Did ye hear that, souls?' Mr Penny said, in a groaning breath.

'Brazen-faced hussies!' said Bowman.

'True; why, they were every note as loud as we, fiddles and all, if not louder!'

'Fiddles and all!' echoed Bowman bitterly.

'Shall anything saucier be found than united 'ooman?' Mr Spinks murmured.

'What I want to know is,' said the tranter (as if he knew already, but that civilization required the form of words), 'what business people have to tell maidens to sing like that when they don't sit in a gallery, and never have entered one in their lives? That's the question, my sonnies.'

' 'Tis the gallery have got to sing, all the world knows,' said Mr Penny. 'Why, souls, what's the use o' the ancients spending scores of pounds to build galleries if people down in the lowest depths of the church sing like that at a moment's notice?'

'Really, I think we useless ones had better march out of church, fiddles and all!' said Mr Spinks, with a laugh which, to a stranger, would have sounded mild and real. Only the initiated body of men he addressed could understand the horrible bitterness of irony that lurked under the quiet words 'useless ones,' and the ghastliness of the laughter apparently so natural.

'Never mind! Let 'em sing too – 'twill make it all the louder – hee, hee!' said Leaf.

'Thomas Leaf, Thomas Leaf! Where have you lived all your life?' said grandfather William sternly.

The quailing Leaf tried to look as if he had lived nowhere at all.

'When all's said and done, my sonnies,' Reuben said, 'there'd have been no real harm in their singing if they had let nobody hear 'em, and only jined in now and then.'

'None at all," said Mr Penny. 'But though I don't wish to accuse people wrongfully, I'd say before my lord judge that I could hear every note o' that last psalm come from 'em as much as from us – every note as if 'twas their own.'

'Know it! ah, I should think I did know it!' Mr Spinks was heard to observe at this moment, without reference to his fellow players – shaking his head at some idea he seemed to see floating before him, and smiling as if he were attending a funeral at the time. 'Ah, do I or don't I know it!'

No one said 'Know what?' because all were aware from experience that what he knew would declare itself in process of time.

'I could fancy last night that we should have some trouble wi' that young man,' said the tranter, pending the continuance of Spinks's speech, and looking towards the unconscious Mr Maybold in the pulpit.

'I fancy,' said old William, rather severely, 'I fancy there's too much whispering going on to be of any spiritual use to gentle or simple.' Then folding his lips and concentrating his glance on the vicar, he implied that none but the ignorant would speak again; and accordingly there was silence in the gallery, Mr Spinks's telling speech remaining for ever unspoken.

Dick had said nothing, and the tranter little, on this

episode of the morning; for Mrs Dewy at breakfast expressed it as her intention to invite the youthful leader of the culprits to the small party it was customary with them to have on Christmas night – a piece of knowledge which had given a particular brightness to Dick's reflections since he had received it. And in the tranter's slightly-cynical nature, party feeling was weaker than in the other members of the choir, though friendliness and faithful partnership still sustained in him a hearty earnestness on their account.

A Christmas Tree

Charles Dickens

I have been looking on, this evening, at a merry company of children assembled round that pretty German toy, a Christmas Tree. The tree was planted in the middle of a great round table, and towered high above their heads. It was brilliantly lighted by a multitude of little tapers; and everywhere sparkled and glittered with bright objects. There were rosy-cheeked dolls, hiding behind the green leaves; and there were real watches (with movable hands, at least, and an endless capacity of being wound up) dangling from innumerable twigs; there were French-polished tables, chairs, bedsteads, wardrobes, eight-day clocks, and various other articles of domestic furniture (wonderfully made, in tin, at Wolverhampton), perched among the boughs, as if in preparation for some fairy housekeeping; there were jolly, broad-faced little men, much more agreeable in appearance than many real men – and no wonder, for their heads took off, and showed them to be full of sugar-plums; there were fiddles and drums; there were tambourines, books, work-boxes, paint-boxes, sweetmeat-boxes, peep-show boxes, and all kinds of boxes; there were trinkets for the elder girls, far brighter than any grown-up gold and jewels; there were baskets and pincushions in all devices; there were guns, swords, and banners; there were witches standing in enchanted rings of pasteboard, to tell fortunes; there were teetotums, humming-tops, needle-cases, pen-wipers, smelling-bottles, conversation-cards, bouquet-holders; real fruit, made artificially dazzling with gold leaf; imitation apples, pears, and walnuts, crammed with surprises; in short, as a pretty child, before me, delightedly whispered to another pretty child, her bosom friend, 'There was everything, and more.' This motley collection of odd objects, clustering on the tree like magic fruit, and flashing back the bright looks directed towards it from every side – some of the diamond-eyes admiring it were hardly on a level with the table, and a few were languishing in timid wonder on the bosoms of pretty mothers, aunts, and nurses – made a lively realisation of the fancies of childhood; and set me thinking how all the trees that grow and all the things that come into existence on the earth, have their wild adornments at that well-remembered time.

Being now at home again, and alone, the only person in the house awake, my thoughts are drawn back, by a fascination which I do not care to resist, to my own childhood. I begin to consider, what do we all remember best upon the branches of the Christmas Tree of our own young Christmas days, by which we climbed to real life.

Straight, in the middle of the room, cramped in the freedom of its growth by no encircling walls or soon-reached ceiling, a shadowy tree arises; and, looking up into the dreamy brightness of its top – for I observe in this tree the singular property that it appears to grow downward towards the earth – I look into my youngest Christmas recollections!

All toys at first, I find. Up yonder, among the green holly and red berries, is the Tumbler with his hands in his pockets, who wouldn't lie down, but whenever he was put upon the floor, persisted in rolling his fat body about, until he rolled himself still, and brought those lobster eyes of his to bear upon me – when I affected to laugh very much, but in my heart of hearts was extremely doubtful of him. Close beside him is that infernal snuff-box, out of which there sprang a demoniacal Counsellor in a black gown, with an obnoxious head of hair, and a red cloth mouth, wide open, who was not to be endured on any terms, but could not be put away either; for he used suddenly, in a highly magnified state, to fly out of Mammoth Snuff-boxes in dreams, when least expected. Nor is the frog with cobbler's wax on his tail, far off; for there was no knowing where he wouldn't jump; and when he flew over the candle, and came upon one's hand with that spotted back – red on a green ground – he was horrible. The cardboard lady in a blue-silk skirt, who was stood up against the candlestick to dance, and whom I see on the same branch, was milder, and was beautiful; but I can't say as much for the larger cardboard man, who used to be hung against the wall and pulled by a string; there was a sinister expression in that nose of his; and when he got his legs round his neck (which he very often did), he was ghastly, and not a creature to be alone with.

When did that dreadful Mask first look at me? Who put it on, and why was I so frightened that the sight of it is an era in my life? It is not a hideous visage in itself; it is even meant to be droll; why then were its stolid features so intolerable? Surely not because it hid the wearer's face. An apron would have done as much; and though I should have preferred even the apron away, it would not have been absolutely insupportable, like the mask. Was it the immovability of the mask? The doll's face was immovable, but I was not afraid of HER. Perhaps that fixed and set change coming over a real face, infused into my quickened heart some remote suggestion and dread of the universal change that is to come on every face, and make it still? Nothing reconciled me to it. No drummers, from whom proceeded a melancholy chirping on the turning of a handle; no regiment of soldiers, with a mute band, taken out of a box, and fitted, one by one, upon a stiff and lazy little set of lazy-tongs; no old woman, made of wires and a brown-paper composition, cutting up a pie for two small children; could give me a permanent comfort, for a long time. Nor was it any satisfaction to be shown the Mask, and see that it was made of paper, or to have it locked up and be assured that no one wore it. The mere recollection of that fixed face, the mere knowledge of its existence anywhere, was sufficient to awake me in the night all perspiration and horror, with, 'O I know it's coming! O the mask!'

I never wondered what the dear old donkey with the panniers – there he is! was made of, then! His hide was real to the touch, I recollect. And the great black horse with the round red spots all over him – the horse that I could even get upon – I never wondered what had brought him to that strange condition, or thought that such a horse was not commonly seen at Newmarket. The four horses of no colour, next to him, that went into the waggon of cheeses, and could be taken out and stabled under the piano, appear to have bits of fur-tippet for their tails, and other bits for their manes, and to stand on pegs instead of legs, but it was not so when they were brought home for a Christmas present. They were all right, then; neither was their harness unceremoniously nailed into their chests, as appears to be the case now. The tinkling works of the music-cart, I DID find out, to be made of quill tooth-picks and wire; and I always thought that little tumbler in his shirt sleeves, perpetually swarming up one side of a wooden frame, and coming down, head foremost, on the other, rather a weak-minded person – though good-natured; but the Jacob's Ladder, next him, made of little squares of red wood, that went flapping and clattering over one another, each developing a different picture, and the whole enlivened by small bells, was a mighty marvel and a great delight.

Ah! The Doll's house!--of which I was not proprietor, but where I visited. I don't admire the Houses of Parliament half so much as that stone-fronted mansion with real glass windows, and door-steps, and a real balcony

– greener than I ever see now, except at watering places; and even they afford but a poor imitation. And though it DID open all at once, the entire house-front (which was a blow, I admit, as cancelling the fiction of a staircase), it was but to shut it up again, and I could believe. Even open, there were three distinct rooms in it: a sitting-room and bed-room, elegantly furnished, and best of all, a kitchen, with uncommonly soft fire-irons, a plentiful assortment of diminutive utensils – oh, the warming-pan! – and a tin man-cook in profile, who was always going to fry two fish. What Barmecide justice have I done to the noble feasts wherein the set of wooden platters figured, each with its own peculiar delicacy, as a ham or turkey, glued tight on to it, and garnished with something green, which I recollect as moss! Could all the Temperance Societies of these later days, united, give me such a tea-drinking as I have had through the means of yonder little set of blue crockery, which really would hold liquid (it ran out of the small wooden cask, I recollect, and tasted of matches), and which made tea, nectar. And if the two legs of the ineffectual little sugar-tongs did tumble over one another, and want purpose, like Punch's hands, what does it matter? And if I did once shriek out, as a poisoned child, and strike the fashionable company with consternation, by reason of having drunk a little teaspoon, inadvertently dissolved in too hot tea, I was never the worse for it, except by a powder!

Upon the next branches of the tree, lower down, hard by the green roller and miniature gardening-tools, how thick the books begin to hang. Thin books, in themselves, at first, but many of them, and with deliciously smooth covers of bright red or green. What fat black letters to begin with! 'A was an archer, and shot at a frog.' Of course he was. He was an apple-pie also, and there he is! He was a good many things in his time, was A, and so were most of his friends, except X, who had so little

93

versatility, that I never knew him to get beyond Xerxes or Xantippe – like Y, who was always confined to a Yacht or a Yew Tree; and Z condemned for ever to be a Zebra or a Zany. But, now, the very tree itself changes, and becomes a bean-stalk – the marvellous bean-stalk up which Jack climbed to the Giant's house! And now, those dreadfully interesting, double-headed giants, with their clubs over their shoulders, begin to stride along the boughs in a perfect throng, dragging knights and ladies home for dinner by the hair of their heads. And Jack – how noble, with his sword of sharpness, and his shoes of swiftness! Again those old meditations come upon me as I gaze up at him; and I debate within myself whether there was more than one Jack (which I am loth to believe possible), or only one genuine original admirable Jack, who achieved all the recorded exploits.

Good for Christmas-time is the ruddy colour of the cloak, in which – the tree making a forest of itself for her to trip through, with her basket – Little Red Riding-Hood comes to me one Christmas Eve to give me information of the cruelty and treachery of that dissembling Wolf who ate her grandmother, without making any impression on his appetite, and then ate her, after making that ferocious joke about his teeth. She was my first love. I felt that if I could have married Little Red Riding-Hood, I should have known perfect bliss. But, it was not to be; and there was nothing for it but to look out the Wolf in the Noah's Ark there, and put him late in the procession on the table, as a monster who was to be degraded. O the wonderful Noah's Ark! It was not found seaworthy when put in a washing-tub, and the animals were crammed in at the roof, and needed to have their legs well shaken down before they could be got in, even there – and then, ten to one but they began to tumble out at the door, which but imperfectly fastened with a wire latch – but what was THAT against it! Consider the noble fly, a size or two smaller than the elephant: the lady-bird, the butterfly – all triumphs of art! Consider the goose, whose feet were so small, and whose balance was so indifferent, that he usually tumbled forward, and knocked down all the animal creation. Consider Noah and his family, like idiotic tobacco-stoppers; and how the leopard stuck to warm little fingers; and how the tails of the larger animals used gradually to resolve themselves into frayed bits of string!

Hush! Again a forest, and somebody up in a tree – not Robin Hood, not Valentine, not the Yellow Dwarf (I have passed him and all Mother Bunch's wonders, without mention), but an Eastern King with a glittering scimitar and turban. By Allah! two Eastern Kings, for I see another, looking over his shoulder! Down upon the grass, at the tree's foot, lies the full length of a coal-black Giant, stretched asleep, with his head in a lady's lap; and near them is a glass box, fastened with four locks of shining steel, in which he keeps the lady prisoner when he is awake. I see the four keys at his girdle now. The lady makes signs to the two kings in the tree, who softly descend. It is the setting-in of the bright Arabian Nights.

Oh, now all common things become uncommon and enchanted to me. All lamps are wonderful; all rings are talismans. Common flower-pots are full of treasure, with a little earth scattered on the top; trees are for Ali Baba to hide in; beef-steaks are to throw down into the Valley of Diamonds, that the precious stones may stick to them, and be carried by the eagles to their nests, whence the traders, with loud cries, will scare them. Tarts are made, according to the recipe of the Vizier's son of Bussorah, who turned pastrycook after he was set down in his drawers at the gate of Damascus; cobblers are all Mustaphas, and in the habit of sewing up people cut into four pieces, to whom they are taken blind-fold.

Any iron ring let into stone is the entrance to a cave which only waits for the magician, and the little fire, and the necromancy, that will make the earth shake. All the dates imported come from the same tree as that unlucky date, with whose shell the merchant knocked out the eye of the genie's invisible son. All olives are of the stock of that fresh fruit, concerning which the Commander of the Faithful overheard the boy conduct the fictitious trial of the fraudulent olive merchant; all apples are akin to the apple purchased (with two others) from the Sultan's gardener for three sequins, and which the tall black slave stole from the child. All dogs are associated with the dog, really a transformed man, who jumped upon the baker's counter, and put his paw on the piece of bad money. All rice recalls the rice which the awful lady, who was a ghoule, could only peck by grains, because of her nightly feasts in the burial-place. My very rocking-horse, – there he is, with his nostrils turned completely inside-out, indicative of Blood! – should have a peg in his neck, by virtue thereof to fly away with me, as the wooden horse did with the Prince of Persia, in the sight of all his father's Court.

Yes, on every object that I recognise among those upper branches of my Christmas Tree, I see this fairy light! When I wake in bed, at daybreak, on the cold, dark, winter mornings, the white snow dimly beheld, outside, through the frost on the window-pane, I hear Dinarzade. 'Sister, sister, if you are yet awake, I pray you finish the history of the Young King of the Black Islands.' Scheherazade replies, 'If my lord the Sultan will suffer me to live another day, sister, I will not only finish that, but tell you a more wonderful story yet.' Then, the gracious Sultan goes out, giving no orders for the execution, and we all three breathe again.

At this height of my tree I begin to see, cowering among the leaves – it may be born of turkey, or of pudding, or mince pie, or of these many fancies, jumbled with Robinson Crusoe on his desert island, Philip Quarll among the monkeys, Sandford and Merton with Mr. Barlow, Mother Bunch, and the Mask – or it may be the result of indigestion, assisted by imagination and over-doctoring – a prodigious nightmare. It is so exceedingly indistinct, that I don't know why it's frightful – but I know it is. I can only make out that it is an immense array of shapeless things, which appear to be planted on a vast exaggeration of the lazy-tongs that used to bear the toy soldiers, and to be slowly coming close to my eyes, and receding to an immeasurable distance. When it comes closest, it is worse. In connection with it I descry remembrances of winter nights incredibly long; of being sent early to bed, as a punishment for some small offence, and waking in two hours, with a sensation of having been asleep two nights; of the laden hopelessness of morning ever dawning; and the oppression of a weight of remorse.

And now, I see a wonderful row of little lights rise smoothly out of the ground, before a vast green curtain. Now, a bell rings – a magic bell, which still sounds in my ears unlike all other bells – and music plays, amidst a buzz of voices, and a fragrant smell of orange-peel and oil. Anon, the magic bell commands the music to cease, and the great green curtain rolls itself up majestically, and The Play begins! The devoted dog of Montargis avenges the death of his master, foully murdered in the Forest of Bondy; and a humorous Peasant with a red nose and a very little hat, whom I take from this hour forth to my bosom as a friend (I think he was a Waiter or an Hostler at a village Inn, but many years have passed since he and I have met), remarks that the sassigassity of that dog is indeed surprising; and evermore this jocular conceit will live in my remembrance fresh and unfading, overtopping all possible jokes, unto the end of time. Or now, I learn with bitter tears how poor Jane Shore, dressed all in white, and with her brown hair hanging down, went starving through the streets; or how George Barnwell killed the worthiest uncle that ever man had, and was afterwards so sorry for it that he ought to have been let off. Comes swift to comfort me, the Pantomime – stupendous Phenomenon! – when clowns are shot from loaded mortars into the great chandelier, bright constellation that it is; when Harlequins, covered all over with scales of pure gold, twist and sparkle, like amazing fish; when Pantaloon (whom I deem it no irreverence to compare in my own mind to my grandfather) puts red-hot pokers in his pocket, and cries 'Here's somebody coming!' or taxes the Clown with petty larceny, by saying, 'Now, I sawed you do it!' when Everything is capable, with the greatest ease, of being changed into Anything; and 'Nothing is, but thinking makes it so.' Now, too, I perceive my first experience of the dreary sensation – often to return in after-life – of being unable, next day, to get back to the dull, settled world; of wanting to live for ever in the bright atmosphere I have quitted; of doting on the little Fairy, with the wand like a celestial Barber's Pole, and pining for a Fairy immortality along with her. Ah, she comes back, in many shapes, as my eye wanders down the branches of my Christmas Tree, and goes as often, and has never yet stayed by me!

Out of this delight springs the toy-theatre, – there it is, with its familiar proscenium, and ladies in feathers, in the boxes! – and all its attendant occupation with paste and glue, and gum, and water colours, in the getting-up of The Miller and his Men, and Elizabeth, or the Exile of Siberia. In spite of a few besetting accidents and failures (particularly an unreasonable disposition in the respectable Kelmar, and some others, to become faint in the legs, and double up, at exciting points of the drama), a teeming world of fancies so suggestive and all-embracing, that, far below it on my Christmas Tree, I see dark, dirty, real Theatres in the day-time, adorned with these associations as with the freshest garlands of the rarest flowers, and charming me yet.

But hark! The Waits are playing, and they break my childish sleep! What images do I associate with the Christmas music as I see them set forth on the Christmas Tree? Known before all the others, keeping far apart from all the others, they gather round my little bed. An angel, speaking to a group of shepherds in a field; some travellers, with eyes uplifted, following a star; a baby in a manger; a child in a spacious temple, talking with grave men; a solemn figure, with a mild and beautiful face, raising a dead girl by the hand; again, near a city gate, calling back the son of a widow, on his bier, to life; a crowd of people looking through the opened roof of a chamber where he sits, and letting down a sick person on a bed, with ropes; the same, in a tempest, walking on the water to a ship; again, on a sea-shore, teaching a great multitude; again, with a child upon his knee, and other children round; again, restoring sight to the blind, speech to the dumb, hearing to the deaf, health to the sick, strength to the lame, knowledge to the ignorant; again, dying upon a Cross, watched by armed soldiers, a thick darkness coming on, the earth beginning to shake, and only one voice heard, 'Forgive them, for they know not what they do.'

Still, on the lower and maturer branches of the Tree, Christmas associations cluster thick. School-books shut up; Ovid and Virgil silenced; the Rule of Three, with its cool impertinent inquiries, long disposed of; Terence and Plautus acted no more, in an arena of huddled desks and forms, all chipped, and notched, and inked; cricket-bats, stumps, and balls, left higher up, with the smell of trodden grass and the softened noise of shouts in the evening air; the tree is still fresh, still gay. If I no more come home at Christmas-time, there will be boys and girls (thank Heaven!) while the World lasts; and they do! Yonder they dance and play upon the branches of my Tree, God bless them, merrily, and my heart dances and plays too!

And I do come home at Christmas. We all do, or we all should. We all come home, or ought to come home, for a short holiday – the longer, the better – from the great boarding-school, where we are for ever working at our arithmetical slates, to take, and give a rest. As to going a visiting, where can we not go, if we will; where have we not been, when we would; starting our fancy from our Christmas Tree!

Away into the winter prospect. There are many such upon the tree! On, by low-lying, misty grounds, through fens and fogs, up long hills, winding dark as caverns between thick plantations, almost shutting out the sparkling stars; so, out on broad heights, until we stop at last, with sudden silence, at an avenue. The gate-bell has a deep, half-awful sound in the frosty air; the gate swings open on its hinges; and, as we drive up to a great house, the glancing lights grow larger in the windows, and the opposing rows of trees seem to fall solemnly back on either side, to give us place. At intervals, all day, a frightened hare has shot across this whitened turf; or the distant clatter of a herd of deer trampling the hard frost, has, for the minute, crushed the silence too. Their watchful eyes beneath the fern may be shining now, if we could see them, like the icy dewdrops on the leaves; but they are still, and all is still. And so, the lights growing larger, and the trees falling back before us, and closing up again behind us, as if to forbid retreat, we come to the house.

There is probably a smell of roasted chestnuts and other good comfortable things all the time, for we are telling Winter Stories – Ghost Stories, or more shame for us – round the Christmas fire; and we have never stirred, except to draw a little nearer to it. But, no matter for that. We came to the house, and it is an old house, full of great chimneys where wood is burnt on ancient dogs upon the hearth, and grim portraits (some of them with grim legends, too) lower distrustfully from the oaken panels of the walls. We are a middle-aged nobleman, and we make a generous supper with our host and hostess and their guests – it being Christmas-time, and the old house full of company – and then we go to bed. Our room is a very old room. It is hung with tapestry. We don't like the portrait of a cavalier in green, over the fireplace. There are great black beams in the ceiling, and there is a great black bedstead, supported at the foot by two great black figures, who seem to have come off a couple of tombs in the old baronial church in the park, for our particular accommodation. But, we are not a superstitious noble-man, and we don't mind. Well! we dismiss our servant, lock the door, and sit before the fire in our dressing-gown, musing about a great many things. At length we go to bed. Well! we can't sleep. We toss and tumble, and can't sleep. The embers on the hearth burn fitfully and make the room look ghostly. We can't help peeping out over the counterpane, at the two black figures and the cavalier – that wicked-looking cavalier – in green. In the flickering light they seem to advance and retire: which, though we are not by any means a superstitious nobleman, is not agreeable. Well! we get nervous – more and more nervous. We say 'This is very foolish, but we can't stand this; we'll pretend to be ill, and knock up somebody.' Well! we are just going to do it, when the locked door opens, and there comes in a young woman, deadly pale, and with long fair hair, who glides to the fire, and sits down in the chair we have left there, wringing her hands. Then, we notice that her clothes are wet. Our tongue cleaves to the roof of our mouth, and we can't speak; but, we observe her accurately. Her clothes are wet; her long hair is dabbled with moist mud; she is dressed in the fashion of two hundred years ago; and she has at her girdle a bunch of rusty keys. Well! there she sits, and we can't even faint, we are in such a state about it. Presently she gets up, and tries all the locks in the room with the rusty keys, which won't fit one of them; then, she fixes her eyes on the portrait of the cavalier in green, and says, in a low, terrible voice, 'The stags know it!' After that, she wrings her hands again, passes the bedside, and goes out at the door. We hurry on our dressing-gown, seize our pistols (we always travel with pistols), and are following, when we find the door locked. We turn the key, look out into the dark gallery; no one there. We wander away, and try to find our servant. Can't be done. We pace the gallery till daybreak; then return to our deserted room, fall asleep, and are awakened by our servant (nothing ever haunts him) and the shining sun. Well! we make a wretched breakfast, and all the company say we look queer. After breakfast, we go over the house with our host, and then we take him to the portrait of the cavalier in green, and then it all comes out. He was false to a young housekeeper once attached to that family, and famous for her beauty, who drowned herself in a pond, and whose body was discovered, after a long time, because the stags refused to drink of the water. Since which, it has been whispered that she traverses the house at midnight (but goes especially to that room where the cavalier in green was wont to sleep), trying the old locks with the rusty keys. Well! we tell our host of what we have seen, and a shade comes over his features, and he begs it may be hushed up; and so it is. But, it's all true; and we said so, before we died (we are dead now) to many responsible people.

There is no end to the old houses, with resounding galleries, and dismal state-bedchambers, and haunted wings shut up for many years, through which we may ramble, with an agreeable creeping up our back, and encounter any number of ghosts, but (it is worthy of remark perhaps) reducible to a very few general types and classes; for, ghosts have little originality, and 'walk' in a beaten track. Thus, it comes to pass, that a certain room in a certain old hall, where a certain bad lord, baronet, knight, or gentleman, shot himself, has certain planks in the floor from which the blood WILL NOT be taken out. You may scrape and scrape, as the present owner has done, or plane and plane, as his father did, or scrub and scrub, as his grandfather did, or burn and burn with strong acids, as his great-grandfather did, but, there the blood will still be – no redder and no paler – no more and no less – always just the same. Thus, in such another house there is a haunted door, that never will keep open; or another door that never will keep shut, or a haunted sound of a spinning-wheel, or a hammer, or a footstep, or a cry, or a sigh, or a horse's tramp, or the rattling of a chain. Or else, there is a turret-clock, which, at the midnight hour, strikes thirteen when the head of the family is going to die; or a shadowy, immovable black carriage which at such a time is always seen by somebody, waiting near the great gates in the stable-yard. Or thus, it came to pass how Lady Mary went to pay a visit at a large wild house in the Scottish Highlands, and, being fatigued with her long journey, retired to bed early, and innocently said, next morning, at the breakfast-table, 'How odd, to have so late a party last night, in this remote place, and not to tell me of it, before I went to bed!' Then, every one asked Lady Mary what she meant? Then, Lady Mary replied, 'Why, all night long, the carriages were driving round and round the terrace, underneath my window!' Then, the owner of the house turned pale, and so did his Lady, and Charles Macdoodle of Macdoodle signed to Lady Mary to say no more, and every one was silent. After breakfast, Charles Macdoodle told Lady Mary that it was a tradition in the family that those rumbling carriages on the terrace betokened death. And so it proved, for, two months afterwards, the Lady of the mansion died. And Lady Mary, who was a Maid of Honour at Court, often told this story to the old Queen

Charlotte; by this token that the old King always said, 'Eh, eh? What, what? Ghosts, ghosts? No such thing, no such thing!' And never left off saying so, until he went to bed.

Or, a friend of somebody's whom most of us know, when he was a young man at college, had a particular friend, with whom he made the compact that, if it were possible for the Spirit to return to this earth after its separation from the body, he of the twain who first died, should reappear to the other. In course of time, this compact was forgotten by our friend; the two young men having progressed in life, and taken diverging paths that were wide asunder. But, one night, many years afterwards, our friend being in the North of England, and staying for the night in an inn, on the Yorkshire Moors, happened to look out of bed; and there, in the moonlight, leaning on a bureau near the window, steadfastly regarding him, saw his old college friend! The appearance being solemnly addressed, replied, in a kind of whisper, but very audibly, 'Do not come near me. I am dead. I am here to redeem my promise. I come from another world, but may not disclose its secrets!' Then, the whole form becoming paler, melted, as it were, into the moonlight, and faded away.

Or, there was the daughter of the first occupier of the picturesque Elizabethan house, so famous in our neighbourhood. You have heard about her? No! Why, SHE went out one summer evening at twilight, when she was a beautiful girl, just seventeen years of age, to gather flowers in the garden; and presently came running, terrified, into the hall to her father, saying, 'Oh, dear father, I have met myself!' He took her in his arms, and told her it was fancy, but she said, 'Oh no! I met myself in the broad walk, and I was pale and gathering withered flowers, and I turned my head, and held them up!' And, that night, she died; and a picture of her story was begun, though never finished, and they say it is somewhere in the house to this day, with its face to the wall.

Or, the uncle of my brother's wife was riding home on horseback, one mellow evening at sunset, when, in a green lane close to his own house, he saw a man standing before him, in the very centre of a narrow way. 'Why does that man in the cloak stand there!' he thought. 'Does he want me to ride over him?' But the figure never moved. He felt a strange sensation at seeing it so still, but slackened his trot and rode forward. When he was so close to it, as almost to touch it with his stirrup, his horse shied, and the figure glided up the bank, in a curious, unearthly manner – backward, and without seeming to use its feet – and was gone. The uncle of my brother's wife, exclaiming, 'Good Heaven! It's my cousin Harry, from Bombay!' put spurs to his horse, which was suddenly in a profuse sweat, and, wondering at such strange behaviour, dashed round to the front of his house. There, he saw the same figure, just passing in at the long French window of the drawing-room, opening on the ground. He threw his bridle to a servant, and hastened in after it. His sister was sitting there, alone. 'Alice, where's my cousin Harry?' 'Your cousin Harry, John?' 'Yes. From Bombay. I met him in the lane just now, and saw him enter here, this instant.' Not a creature had been seen by any one; and in that hour and minute, as it afterwards appeared, this cousin died in India.

Or, it was a certain sensible old maiden lady, who died at ninety-nine, and retained her faculties to the last, who really did see the Orphan Boy; a story which has often been incorrectly told, but, of which the real truth is this – because it is, in fact, a story belonging to our family – and she was a connexion of our family. When she was about forty years of age, and still an uncommonly fine woman (her lover died young, which was the reason why she never married, though she had many offers), she went to stay at a place in Kent, which her brother, an Indian-Merchant, had newly bought. There was a story that this place had once been held in trust by the guardian of a young boy; who was himself the next heir, and who killed the young boy by harsh and cruel treatment. She knew nothing of that. It has been said that there was a Cage in her bedroom in which the guardian used to put the boy. There was no such thing. There was only a closet. She went to bed, made no alarm whatever in the night, and in the morning said composedly to her maid when she came in, 'Who is the pretty forlorn-looking child who has been peeping out of that closet all night?' The maid replied by giving a loud scream, and instantly decamping. She was surprised; but she was a woman of remarkable strength of mind, and she dressed herself and went downstairs, and closeted herself with her brother. 'Now, Walter,' she said, 'I have been disturbed all night by a pretty, forlorn-looking boy, who has been constantly peeping out of that closet in my room, which I can't open. This is some trick.' 'I am afraid not, Charlotte,' said he, 'for it is the legend of the house. It is the Orphan Boy. What did he do?' 'He opened the door softly,' said she, 'and peeped out. Sometimes, he came a step or two into the room. Then, I called to him, to encourage him, and he shrunk, and shuddered, and crept in again, and shut the door.' 'The closet has no communication, Charlotte,' said her brother, 'with any other part of the house, and it's nailed up.' This was undeniably true, and it took two carpenters a whole forenoon to get it open, for examination. Then, she was satisfied that she had seen the Orphan Boy. But, the wild and terrible part of the story is, that he was also seen by three of her brother's sons, in succession, who all died young. On the occasion of each child being taken ill, he came home in a heat, twelve hours before, and said, Oh, Mamma, he had been playing under a particular oak-tree, in a certain meadow, with a strange boy – a pretty, forlorn-looking boy, who was very timid, and made signs! From fatal experience, the parents came to know that this was the Orphan Boy, and that the course of that child whom he chose for his little playmate was surely run.

Legion is the name of the German castles, where we sit up alone to wait for the Spectre – where we are shown into a room, made comparatively cheerful for our reception – where we glance round at the shadows, thrown on the blank walls by the crackling fire – where we feel very lonely when the village innkeeper and his pretty daughter have retired, after laying down a fresh store of wood upon the hearth, and setting forth on the small table such supper-cheer as a cold roast capon, bread, grapes, and a flask of old Rhine wine – where the reverberating doors close on their retreat, one after another, like so many peals of sullen thunder – and where, about the small hours of the night, we come into the knowledge of divers supernatural mysteries. Legion is the name of the haunted German students, in whose society we draw yet nearer to the fire, while the schoolboy in the corner opens his eyes wide and round, and flies off the footstool he has chosen for his seat, when the door accidentally blows open. Vast is the crop of such fruit, shining on our Christmas Tree; in blossom, almost at the very top; ripening all down the boughs!

Among the later toys and fancies hanging there – as idle often and less pure –be the images once associated with the sweet old Waits, the softened music in the night, ever unalterable! Encircled by the social thoughts of Christmas-time, still let the benignant figure of my childhood stand unchanged! In every cheerful image and suggestion that the season brings, may the bright star that rested above the poor roof, be the star of all the Christian World! A moment's pause, O vanishing tree, of which the lower boughs are dark to me as yet, and let me look once more! I know there are blank spaces on thy branches, where eyes that I have loved have shone and smiled; from which they are departed. But, far above, I see the raiser of the dead girl, and the Widow's Son; and God is good! If Age be hiding for me in the unseen portion of thy downward growth, O may I, with a grey head, turn a child's heart to that figure yet, and a child's trustfulness and confidence!

Now, the tree is decorated with bright merriment, and song, and dance, and cheerfulness. And they are welcome. Innocent and welcome be they ever held, beneath the branches of the Christmas Tree, which cast no gloomy shadow! But, as it sinks into the ground, I hear a whisper going through the leaves. 'This, in commemoration of the law of love and kindness, mercy and compassion. This, in remembrance of Me!'

Poetry

If Jesus was born today

If Jesus was born today
it would be in a downtown motel
marked by a helicopter's flashing bulb.
A traffic warden, working late,
would be the first upon the scene.
Later, at the expense of a TV network,
an eminent sociologist,
the host of a chat show
and a controversial author
would arrive with their good wishes
– the whole occasion to be filmed as part of the
'Is This The Son Of God?' one hour special.
Childhood would be a blur of photographs and speculation
dwindling by his late teens into
'Where Is He Now?' features in Sunday magazines.

If Jesus was thirty today
they wouldn't really care about the public ministry,
they'd be too busy investigating His finances
and trying to prove He had Church or Mafia connections.
The miracles would be explained by
an eminent and controversial magician,
His claims to be God's Son recognised as
excellent examples of Spoken English
and immediately incorporated into
the O-Level syllabus,
His sinless perfection considered by moral philosophers
as, OK, but a bit repressive.

If Jesus was thirty-one today
He'd be the fly in everyone's ointment –

the sort of controversial person who
stands no chance of eminence.
Communists would expel Him, capitalists
would exploit Him or have Him
smeared by people who know a thing or two about God.
Doctors would accuse Him of quackery,
soldiers would accuse Him of cowardice,
theologians would take Him aside and try
to persuade Him of His non-existence.

If Jesus was thirty-two today we'd have to
end it all. Heretic, fundamentalist, literalist,
puritan, pacifist, non-conformist, we'd take Him
away and quietly end the argument.
But the argument would rumble in the ground
at the end of three days and would break out
and walk around as though death was some bug,
saying 'I am the resurrection and the life…
No man cometh to the Father but by me'.
While the magicians researched new explanations
and the semanticists wondered exactly what
He meant by 'I' and 'No man' there would be those
who stand around amused, asking for something
called proof.

STEVE TURNER

From The Liturgy of St James

Let all mortal flesh keep silence,
And with fear and trembling stand;
Ponder nothing earthly minded,
For with blessing in His hand,
Christ our God to earth descendeth,
Our full homage to demand.

King of kings, yet born of Mary,
As of old on earth He stood,
Lord of lords, in human vesture,
In the body and the blood;
He will give to all the faithful
His own self for heavenly food.

Rank on rank the host of heaven
Spreads its vanguard on the way,
As the Light of light descendeth
From the realms of endless day,
That the powers of hell may vanish
As the darkness clears away.

At His feet the six wingèd seraph,
Cherubim with sleepless eye,
Veil their faces to the presence,
As with ceaseless voice they cry:
Alleluia, Alleluia
Alleluia, Lord Most High!

translated from the Greek by GERARD MOULTRIE
Original: 4th century

Music on Christmas Morning

Music I love – but never strain
Could kindle raptures so divine,
So grief assuage, so conquer pain,
And rouse this pensive heart of mine –
As that we hear on Christmas morn,
Upon the wintry breezes borne.

Though Darkness still her empire keep,
And hours must pass, ere morning break;
From troubled dreams, or slumbers deep,
That music KINDLY bids us wake:
It calls us, with an angel's voice,
To wake, and worship, and rejoice;

To greet with joy the glorious morn,
Which angels welcomed long ago,
When our redeeming Lord was born,
To bring the light of Heaven below;
The Powers of Darkness to dispel,
And rescue Earth from Death and Hell.

While listening to that sacred strain,
My raptured spirit soars on high;
I seem to hear those songs again
Resounding through the open sky,
That kindled such divine delight,
In those who watched their flocks by night.

With them I celebrate His birth –
Glory to God, in highest Heaven,
Good-will to men, and peace on earth,
To us a Saviour-king is given;
Our God is come to claim His own,
And Satan's power is overthrown!

A sinless God, for sinful men,
Descends to suffer and to bleed;
Hell MUST renounce its empire then;
The price is paid, the world is freed,
And Satan's self must now confess
That Christ has earned a RIGHT to bless:

Now holy Peace may smile from heaven,
And heavenly Truth from earth shall spring:
The captive's galling bonds are riven,
For our Redeemer is our king;
And He that gave his blood for men
Will lead us home to God again.

ANNE BRONTË

Adam lay ybounden

Adam lay ybounden, bounden in a bond,
Four thousand winter thought he not too long;
And all was for an apple, and apple that he took,
As clerkes finden writen, writen in hire book.
Ne hadde the apple taken been, the apple taken been,
Ne hadde nevere Oure Lady ybeen hevene Queen.
Blessed be the time that apple taken was:
Therfore we mown singen *Deo Gratias.*

hire: their
Ne hadde: had not
mown: must
Deo Gratias: thanks be to God

ANONYMOUS
c. 1430

A Christmas Ghost-Story

South of the Line, inland from far Durban,
A mouldering soldier lies – your countryman.
Awry and doubled up are his grey bones,
And on the breeze his puzzled phantom moans
Nightly to clear Canopus: 'I would know
By whom and when the All-Earth-gladdening Law
Of peace, brought in by that Man Crucified,
Was ruled to be inept, and set aside?
And what of logic or of truth appears
In tacking "Anno Domini" to the years?
Near twenty-hundred liveried thus have hied,
But tarries yet the Cause for which He died.'

THOMAS HARDY
Christmas Eve, 1899

The poem was written at the time of the Boer War

The Little Match Girl

William Topaz McGonagall (1825 – 1902) is widely regarded as the worst poet in the world.
Here is an example of his work.

It was biting cold, and the falling snow,
Which filled a poor little match girl's heart with woe,
Who was bareheaded and barefooted, as she went along
                    the street,
Crying, 'Who'll buy my matches? for I want pennies to buy
                    some meat!'

When she left home she had slippers on;
But, alas! poor child, now they were gone.
For she lost both of them while hurrying across the street,
Out of the way of two carriages which were near by her
                    feet.

So the little girl went on, while the snow fell thick and fast;
And the child's heart felt cold and downcast,
For nobody had bought any matches that day,
Which filled her little mind with grief and dismay.

Alas! she was hungry and shivering with cold;
So in a corner between two houses she made bold
To take shelter from the violent storm.
Poor little waif! wishing to herself she'd never been born.

And she grew colder and colder, and feared to go home
For fear of her father beating her; and she felt woe-begone
Because she could carry home no pennies to buy bread,
And to go home without pennies she was in dread.

The large flakes of snow covered her ringlets of fair hair;
While the passers-by for her had no care,
As they hurried along to their homes at a quick pace,
While the cold wind blew in the match girl's face.

As night wore on her hands were numb with cold,
And no longer her strength could her uphold,
When an idea into her little head came:
She'd strike a match and warm her hands at the flame.

And she lighted the match, and it burned brightly,
And it helped to fill her heart with glee;
And she thought she was sitting at a stove very grand;
But, alas! she was found dead, with a match in her hand!

Her body was found half-covered with snow,
And as the people gazed thereon their hearts were full of
                                                woe;
And many present let fall a burning tear
Because she was found dead on the last night of the year,

In that mighty city of London, wherein is plenty of gold –
But, alas! their charity towards street waifs is rather cold.
But I hope the match girl's in Heaven, beside her Saviour
                                                dear,
A bright reward for all the hardships she suffered here.

WILLIAM MCGONAGALL

The Darkling Thrush

I leant upon a coppice gate
   When Frost was spectre-grey,
And Winter's dregs made desolate
   The weakening eye of day.
The tangled bine-stems scored the sky
   Like strings of broken lyres,
And all mankind that haunted nigh
   Had sought their household fires.

The land's sharp features seemed to be
   The Century's corpse outleant,
His crypt the cloudy canopy,
   The wind his death-lament.
The ancient pulse of germ and birth
   Was shrunken hard and dry,
And every spirit upon earth
   Seemed fervourless as I.

At once a voice arose among
   The bleak twigs overhead
In a full-hearted evensong
   Of joy illimited;
An aged thrush, frail, gaunt and small,
   In blast-beruffled plume,
Had chosen thus to fling his soul
   Upon the growing gloom.

So little cause for carolings
    Of such ecstatic sound
Was written on terrestrial things
    Afar or nigh around,
That I could think there trembled through
    His happy good-night air
Some blessed Hope, whereof he knew
    And I was unaware.

THOMAS HARDY

The Chester Mystery Plays

The Nativity

Mystery Plays were common in Britain until they were banned at the Reformation. This is the text of the beginning of the Nativity play from the Chester cycle. The writers were anonymous, though the plays appear to be the product of a monastery.

For clarity, some spelling has been modernised.

GABRIEL

Hail be thou, Mary, mother free,
full of grace. God is with thee.
Amongst all women blessed thou be,
and the fruit of thy body.

MARY

Ah, lord that sittes high in see,   *see: seat*
that wondrously now mervayles me –
a simple maiden of my degree be
greet this graciously.

GABRIEL

Mary, ne dread thee nought this case.   *ne: not*
With great God found thou hase
amongst all other special grace.
Therefore, Mary, thou mone   *mone: must*

conceive and bear – I tell thee –
a childe. Jesus his name shall be –
so great shall never none be as he –
and called Goddes Sonne.
And our Lord God, lieve thou me,   *lieve: allow*
shall give him David his father's see;
in Jacob's howse reigning shall he
with full might evermore.
And he that shall be borne of thee,
endless life in him shall be,
that such renown and royalty
had never none before.

MARY

How may this be, thou beast so bright?
In sin know I no worldly wight.   *wight: person*

GABRIEL

The Holy Ghost shall in thee light
from God in majesty,
and shadow thee, seemly in sight.
Therefore that holy one, as I have height   *height: called*
that thou shalt bear through Goddes might,
he Sonne shall called be.
Elizabeth that barren was
as thou may see conceived has
in age a sonne through Goddes grace,
the [babe] shall be of blysse.
The sixte moneth is gone now again
seeth men called her barren;   *seeth: since*
but nothinge to Goddes might and mayne
impossible is.

MARY

Now syth that God will it so be,   *syth: since*
and such grace hath sent to me,
blessed evermore be he;
to please him I am payde.   *payde: satisfied, pleased*
Lo, Goddes chosen meekely here –
and Lord God, prince of powere,
leave that it fall in suche mannere
this word that thou hast said.

Exit Gabriel, enter Elizabeth.

Elizabeth, nece, God thee see.   *nece: niece, i.e. kinswoman*

ELIZABETH

Mary, blessed mote thou be,   *mote: must*
and the fruites that commes of thee,
amonge women all.
Wonderly now mervayles me
that Marye, Goddes mother free,
greetes me thus of simple degree.
Lord, how may this befall?
When thou me greetest, sweet Marye,
the childe stirred in my bodye
for great joye of thy companye
and the fruite that is in thee.
Blessed be thou ever forthy,
that lived so well and stedfastly;
for that was saide to thee, ladye,
fulfilled and done shall be.

MARY

Elizabeth, therefore will I

thank the lord, kinge of mercye,
with joyful myrth and melody
and laud to his likinge.
'Magnificat,' while I have toome,
'anima mea dominum'
to Christ that in my kind is come,
devoutly I will singe.
And for my ghost joyed hase
 in God, my heale and all my grace –
for meekenes he see in me was,
his feere of meane degree –
therfore blesse me well maye
all generations for aye.
Much has that Lord done for me,
that moste is in his majesty.
Therefore with full heart and free
his name alway hallowed be;
and honoured evermore be he
one height in heaven blisse.
Much has God done for me today;
his name aye hollowed be,
as he is bound to do mercy
from progeny to progeny.
And all that dredene him verily,
his talent to fulfil,
be through his might gave maystery.
Disparcles proud dispytuusly
with myght of his harte hastely
at his owne will.
Deposeth mighty out of place,
and milde also he hansed hasse;
hungry, needy, wanting grace
With God he hath fullfillede.
That rich power he hath forsaken;
To Iserael, his Sonne he hath betakene.
And mercy hasse of his guilte –

Magnificat anima mea dominum: 'My soul magnifies the Lord' – the song of Mary from Luke 1.46ff. 'Toome' is 'leisure'.

heale: salvation

feere: companion

dredene: fear

i.e. he scatters the proud, angrily

hansed: exalted

125

as he spake to our fathers before,
Abrahame and his syde full yore.   *syde: seed*
Joy to the Father evermore,
the Sonne, and the Holy Ghoste,
as was from the beginninge
and never shall have endinge,
from world to world aye wendinge.
Amen, God of might most.

ELIZABETH

Marye, now redd I that we gone   *redd: advise*
to Joseph thy husband anon,
lesse he to misse thee make mone;
for now that is moste neede.

MARY

Elizabeth, nece, to do so good is,   *nece: niece, i.e. kinswoman*
leste be suppose one mea amysse;
but good Lord that hath ordayned this
will witness of my deede.

ELIZABETH

Joseph, God thee save and see!
Thy wife here I brought to thee.

JOSEPH

Alas, alas, and woe is me!
Who hasse made her with chyld?
Well I wist an ould man and a maye   *wist: know*
might not accord by no waye.   *maye: young woman*
For many yeares might I not playe
ne worke no workes wild.

126

Now hasse she gotten her, as I see,
a great bellye like to thee
syth she went away.
And mine it is not, be thou bold,
for I am both old and cold;
these thirty winters, though
I would, I might not play no play.
Alas, where might I lenge or lende?   *lenge or lende: linger or stay*
For loth is me my wife to shende,   *shende: disgrace*
therfore from her will I wende
into some other place.
For to dyscreeve will I nought,   *dyscreeve: disgrace*
feeblye though she have wrought.   *feebly: weakly*
To leave her privelye is my thought,   *privelye: privately*
that no man know this case.
God, let never an old man
take to wife a yonge woman
ney seet his hearte her upon,
lest he beguiled be.
For accorde there may be none,
ney they may never be at one;
and that is seene in manye one
as well as one: me.
Therfore have I slept a while,
my wife that me can thus beguile,
for I will gone from her; it to fyle   *it to file: to make her worthless*
me is loth, in good faye.   *faye: faith*
This case makes me so heavye
that needes sleepe nowe muste I.
Lord, on her thou have mercye
for her misdeede todaye.

ANGEL

Joseph, let be thy feeble thought.
Take Marye thy wife and dread thee nought,

127

for wickedly she hath not wrought;
but this is Goddes will.
The child that she shall beare, iwys   *iwys: I know*
of the Holy Ghost begotten it is
to save mankynd that did amisse,
and prophecye to fulfill.

JOSEPH

A, nowe I wot, lord, it is so,   *wot: know*
I will no man be her foe;
but while I may on yearth go,   *yearth: earth*
with her I will be.
Nowe Christe is in our kynde light,
as the prophetes before hight.   *hight: called*
Lord God, most of might,
with weale I worship thee.   *weale: happiness*

128

All the trimmings

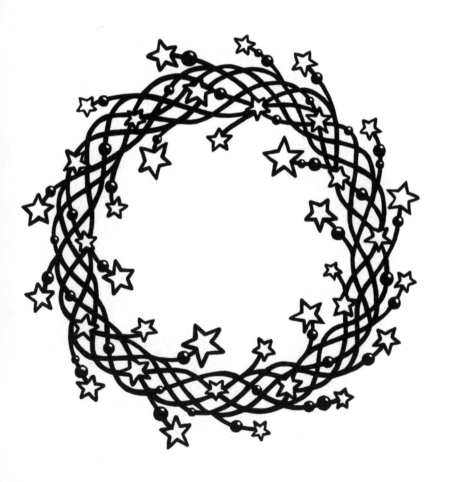

Present day costs for all the gifts mentioned in
The Twelve Days of Christmas

1. Single partridge + single pear tree.

A Beth pear tree from an online nursery in Somerset costs £11.25 plus £6.50 delivery, so that's £17.75.

We'll assume a live partridge rather than a dead one is required. (An oven-ready partridge stuck on a polystyrene tray and wrapped in plastic might look a bit odd when nailed to a tree, although perhaps it's no more bizarre than some of the other presents ordered by 'my true love', who is clearly a most eccentric individual.) We found a live single partridge online for £80, called a *sindi thithria* (this is the name of the breed; it's not an example of a popular range of dolls). Presumably you'd have to pick it up; it'd be hard to send by Royal Mail. So, let's say the partridge would cost £80 and we'll ignore any mileage costs.

Apparently, most breeds of partridge do not like to perch in trees. You will, however, be relieved to hear that the red legged partridge does occasionally do so – though we can't find a price for one of these, so it'll have to be a *sindi thithria*. Let's hope they like pear trees.

Total cost of a partridge in a pear tree: £97.75.

2. Turtle doves, one pair.

Again, we'll assume live ones are required. We could only find plastic ones on eBay, so that's not much good.

Real turtle doves are not very easy to find. If my true love were looking for garden fantail doves or Indian fantails, life would be a lot easier. An additional problem, according to birdchannel.com, is that turtle doves are terrified of human beings. However, they eat a lot of snails, so they'd be useful in your garden.

The UK population of turtle doves has fallen by more than 84% since 1970, so the pair required would have to be sourced from overseas. We found a breeder in the US who'll supply them for $75 per pair (=£46.34 at the time of writing). The best way to get them to the UK would be to have them flown over in an aeroplane, accompanied by a responsible adult (we'll assume the cooing avian pets might just be allowed as hand luggage). So, say £450 for the airline ticket and then you collect them from the airport to save on any other transport costs.

(Note: the song keeps on listing all the presents received thus far. We make the assumption that, when it does so, it is just recollecting the munificence of previous days, and is not detailing yet more gifts of partridges in pear trees, additional turtle doves, supplementary French hens or whatever given on subsequent days (otherwise you'd end up with twelve patridges, twelve pear trees, 22 turtle doves and so on, and that would just be silly).)

Total cost of two turtle doves: £496.34

Running total: £594.09

3. Three French hens.

There doesn't seem to be a breed as such called a 'French hen'. There are, though, a number of French breeds of hen. One of the most popular is the faverolle and there's a supplier in Dorset who'll sell you a 10 week old bird for £25. Let's ignore transport costs on this one. We need three of them.

Total cost: £75

Running total: £669.09

4. Four calling birds

Actually, it should be 'colly' birds: blackbirds. These are pretty common and there's little need to buy them. We'll assume a net, some bird seed and a lot of patience will do the trick. Say £3.50 for the bird seed and £5 for a suitable net. (NB: don't try this or you'll end up in court.)

Total for four calling birds: £8.50.
(One of the cheaper items!)

Running total: £677.59

5. Five gold rings.

Sky's the limit here. You can get rings with white gold in them (probably *not very much* gold) on eBay from 1p upwards, but let's assume this is a bit basic. The lowest price for a solid gold ring seems to be about £65, so five of these would set you back £325.

Total for five gold rings: £325

Running total: £1002.59

6. Six geese a-laying

Presumably, this means six geese who are capable of laying, rather than six geese who are in the process of laying. It would be very hard to find six geese who were all about to pop at the same instant on 30th December. You can get an adult goose on Preloved for twenty quid, so let's say:

Total for six geese a-laying: £120.
(NB: you'd need to factor in shelter, food and so on, which we haven't done.)

Running total: £1122.59

7. Seven swans a-swimming.

Right. This one's a problem.

Swans belong to Her Majesty the Queen and you can't pinch them. Actually, this isn't quite true: HM only owns unmarked swans: the ones with no markings on their beaks. Swans with markings on the right side of their beaks belong to the Worshipful Company of Dyers (why?) and swans with a mark on both sides of their beaks belong to the Vintners' Company (*why??*).

We rang the RSPB for their advice; they said you can't buy swans in the UK, though they agreed it would be OK for you to possess a watercourse and then hope that seven swans a-swimming might turn up.

As such a fortuitous and random arrival seems pretty unlikely, the best bet would seem to be to find a bloke in a pub who's willing to snaffle some swans for you, preferably under the cover of darkness.

In Queen Elizabeth I's time, you could get a year in the Tower for stealing one of her swans; the penalty today for harming or killing a swan is a fine of £5000 or six months inside. Abducting one of these graceful birds thus carries the risk not only of doing bird (ha ha), but of being savagely pecked, which might mean one or more swans runs the risk of being injured as their abductor defends himself from their violent but quite reasonable objection to being kidnapped. All this means danger money would have to be paid to your dodgy partner in crime, but we think £1000 in used tenners might do it.

(Note: don't try it. Swans are beautiful birds and you should leave them alone.)

(Another note: this one demonstrates that my true love was not only eccentric but also criminal in his purchasing choices.)

Total for seven swans a-swimming: £1000.

Running total: £2122.59.

8. Eight maids a-milking.

Let's suppose my true love, in additional to being a criminal eccentric, is also parsimonious and doesn't want to pay the ladies any more than he has to. Let's also suppose all eight maids are over 21 years old. The minimum wage for persons over 21 years of age is £6.08 per hour. We assume the cows are already there (possibly pasturing between the pear tree and the seven swans a-swimming) and that two hours' milking is required from each maid. 8 x 2 x £6.08 = £97.28.

Total for eight maids a-milking: £97.28

Running total: £2219.87

9. Nine ladies dancing.

Equity advises that a ballet dancer should be paid a minimum of £347 per week. Let's assume a week of five days; that's £69.40 per day. Multiply by nine and you get £624.60.

Total for nine ladies dancing: £624.60.

Running total: £2844.47.

10. Ten lords a-leaping.

Why you should want ten lords a-leaping is anybody's guess. Pricing it is difficult. Let's base it on the House of Lords attendance allowance, as their lordships should be willing to do a bit of jumping about for a day for the same rate.

The attendance allowance for the House of Lords varies but a basic rate of £150 per day may be claimed. That means £1500 for ten lords.

Question: how to induce their lordships to undertake said a-leaping foolishness?

A possibly answer is to place a large gin and tonic behind a hurdle, one for each lord. You will therefore need to have ten hurdles and ten G and Ts. In order to reach his gin and tonic, each lord must leap over his hurdle.

Two one-litre bottles of Gordon's gin cost a total of about £44. Say £6 for the tonic water and lemons or limes. £50 so far.

We found some 12 inch hurdles for £7.99 each on eBay (free delivery). Ten are needed, so that's £79.90.

Total for ten lords a-leaping: £1629.90

Running total: £4474.37.

11. Eleven pipers piping.

The Musicians' Union standard audio session fee for a non-classical recording is £120, so that would seem about right for each piper who is required to undertake piping. £120 x 11 = £1320.

Total for eleven pipers piping: £1320.

Running total: £5794.37.

12. Twelve drummers drumming.

Taking the same rate as the eleven pipers piping, this would set you back £1440.

Total for twelve drummers drumming: £1440.

Thus we conclude that the total cost to my true love for his or her Christmas munificence is:

£7234.37.

Twelve things you didn't know about
The Twelve Days of Christmas

1. *The Twelve Days of Christmas* was first published in English in 1780.
2. It may have started life in French as a memory game: person A says a line, person B has to add a second line and repeat the first line, person C adds a third line and has to remember the first two and so on. Anyone who forgets one of them has to pay a forfeit.
3. The order of the gifts varies in different versions. Some have twelve lords a-leaping instead of ten.
4. Or nine drummers drumming instead of twelve.
5. Or ten pipers piping instead of eleven.
6. Four calling birds, as we've seen, were originally four colly birds (blackbirds) and this is sometimes changed to four mockingbirds.
7. The nesting habits of partridges do not usually encompass residence in pear trees. It's therefore suggested that the 'pear tree' may be a corruption of the French *perdix* and the original gift was just one specimen of said wildfowl. Some facetious persons object to this, as you'd end up with 'a partridge in a partridge', which is bizarre.
8. Five gold rings might have originally been five goldspinks, i.e. five goldfinches.
9. Some versions have 'five golden rings' rather than five go-hoooold rings.
10. One French version has twelve musketeers with their swords as a gift. Nasty.
11. A Scottish version includes the gift of an Arabian baboon. It is unknown which shops were purveyors of these anthropoids.
12. Attempts have been made to explain the gifts as Christian symbolism, so the partridge is Jesus; the seven swans a-swimming are the seven gifts of the

Holy Spirit; the ten lords a-leaping are the ten commandments and so on. While this is ingenious, it's not likely to have been the original meaning.

One of the more bizarre Christmas presents offered on Amazon in 2011 was the Sigmund Freud action figure (£14.40 each). There was a variant of this exciting toy: the sky-diving Sigmund Freud action figure.

The explorers Alfred Gibson and Ernest Giles attempted to cross the deserts of Western Australia in the 1870s. For their 1873 Christmas dinner, they ate Christmas pudding and roast wallaby.

More than three billion Christmas cards are sent each year in the United States.

In 2011, the Theos think-tank commissioned an opinion poll to discover people's attitudes to Christmas. It found:

- Almost half agreed with the idea that Christmas is about the traditional Christian message;
- 41% agreed with the statement, 'Christmas is about celebrating that God loves humanity';
- 40% agreed with 'Christmas doesn't really have any meaning today';
- 83% agreed that Christmas is a time to spend with friends and family;
- 62% agreed that Christmas is a time to be generous to the less fortunate;
- 34% said Christmas was a time to tackle poverty and economic injustice
- 33% or so intended to attend a religious service at Christmas.

Snow is rare in Bethlehem at Christmas, though it sometimes happens. Thus Christina Rossetti's 'Snow had fallen, snow on snow, snow on snow' is possible – but she was probably more influenced by the arctic English winters of her day than by detailed knowledge of the Israeli climate. (In any case, celebrating the birth of Jesus on 25th December is a traditional date; the actual day of Jesus' birth is not known.) Snow is more common in December in Galilee than in what was Judea. It doesn't spoil the carol, though: the symbolism's more important than meteorological accuracy...

What was on politicians' Christmas cards in 2011?

Mr and Mrs Cameron's card had a photo of Mr and Mrs Cameron.

Mr and Mrs Miliband's card had a photo of Mr and Mrs Miliband (and their children).

Mr and Mrs Clegg had a picture of snowmen, drawn by their children Antonio and Alberto.

Also of note:

Mr Osborne personally signs 2500 Christmas cards.

Mr Vince Cable did not send any Christmas cards to Tory MPs in 2011.

Mr Gordon Brown's 2009 Christmas card featured a decoration of a tiny 10 Downing Street door hanging from a Christmas tree. *The Guardian*'s cartoonist Martin Rowson offered an alternative version of Mr Brown wishing everyone 'A Very Merry Doonturn!' and saying, 'And doon't forget, kiddies! We'll be taking back all yur presents next year!'

In 1541, Henry VIII banned all sport on Christmas Day.

A female turkey is called a hen.

A trawl of major London retailers revealed the following non-bargain basement children's Christmas gifts for 2011:

- A cashmere baby-gro (ages 3 to 6 months): £550.
- Rocking horse: £5,995.
- Downton Abbey-style doll's house: £899. The furniture and other kit to equip it cost a further £5000.
- Wooden pirate ship (could be adapted as a bed or a desk): £5,995.
- Hand-built Mini Seven car, with petrol engine and a top speed of 19 mph: £9,995.

Traditional Christmas food includes codfish (Brazil), fried fish with potato salad (Czech Republic), roast reindeer (Iceland), and boiled octopus (Portugal). In Lithuania, a twelve dish Christmas dinner is eaten on Christmas Eve; one dish for each of the apostles.

Three kings from Persian lands afar

The wise men or magi who visit the infant Jesus in Matthew's Gospel aren't named by the writer, nor does he say there were three of them (it was later assumed there were because of the three gifts). The point Matthew is making is that it's Gentiles – non-Jews – who visit Christ. This anticipates the Christian message going out from Judaism to the Gentile world, a key theme in Matthew (and indeed in the rest of the New Testament). Luke's Gospel has the (Jewish) shepherds instead, showing that it's for the poor that Christ has come, and for those who, like shepherds, were considered outcasts from polite society. (The hours shepherds kept meant they couldn't participate in normal Jewish religious observances, so they were on the fringes of first century Judaism.)

Some early Christian writers thought that the magi's giving gifts to the infant Jesus showed that they were surrendering the power of making magic in the face of the greater authority of Christ. 'Magi' and 'magic' have the same root and magi in the first century were believed to be wise men – with the 'wisdom' of being able to cast spells.

The names Melchior, Caspar (or Gaspar) and Balthazar seem to date from around 500 AD. These are the names commonly used in Western Christian tradition, though Armenian Christians call them Kagpha, Badadakharida and Badadilma; Syrian Christians have Larvandad, Gushnasaph, and Hormisdas; and many other Eastern Churches call them Hor, Karsudan, and Basanater.

In the 1977 series *Jesus of Nazareth,* the magi are played by Fernando Rey, Donald Pleasence and James Earl Jones. James Earl Jones is better known as Darth Vader and Donald Pleasence has a great pedigree of playing villains, including Ernst Stavro Blofeld, James Bond's nemesis in *You Only Live Twice.*

It is perfectly legal to get married in the UK on Christmas Day. The Church of England will allow you to marry in church... so long as you can find a priest who's able to work around his or her usual Christmas services.

On Christmas Day...

1800 The first (royal) Christmas tree was erected inside the Queen's Lodge at Windsor by Queen Charlotte, wife of George III. (Prince Albert revived the royal Christmas tree but he did not invent it.)

1805 Nelson's body was carried ashore at Greenwich Hospital.

1861 The first version of what became known as *Mrs Beeton's Book of Household Management* was published. Its original title was *The Book of Household Management, comprising information for the Mistress, Housekeeper, Cook, Kitchen-Maid, Butler, Footman, Coachman, Valet, Upper and Under House-Maids, Lady's-Maid, Maid-of-all-Work, Laundry-Maid, Nurse and Nurse-Maid, Monthly Wet and Sick Nurses, etc. etc. – also Sanitary, Medical, & Legal Memoranda: with a History of the Origin, Properties, and Uses of all Things Connected with Home Life and Comfort.*

1871   The first time Christmas Day was a bank holiday in Scotland. (It was already a national holiday in the rest of the UK.)

1878   Birth of Louis Chevrolet, founder of the Chevrolet Motor Car Company.

1887   First distilling of Glenfiddich whisky took place.
        Birth of Conrad Hilton, founder of the hotel chain.

1889   England's first mosque opened in Liverpool.
        Last Mass celebrated by John Henry Newman, who died the following year.

1895   Fifteen RNLI volunteer lifeboatmen were drowned when going to the aid of the SS Palme in Dublin Bay. An annual ecumenical service at Dun Laoghaire still remembers the tragedy, and commemorates all those who lost their lives at sea in the past year.

1898   Penny postage throughout the Empire was introduced – so you could send a letter anywhere in the British Empire for a penny.
        Warmest Christmas day in Armagh, at 12.9° C – until 2010, when it was 13.5°.

1927   By contrast, a 40-hour blizzard began in the UK. Box Hill in Surrey became a temporary ski slope and many Londoners took to their skis to get across the city.

1936   Birth of Princess Alexandra of Kent.

1950   The Stone of Scone was removed from Westminster Abbey by four Scots students, for return to Scotland.

1991   Mikhail Gorbachev declared that his office as President of the USSR no longer existed, as the USSR had ceased to be.

'Happy Holidays!'

'Happy Holidays!' as a greeting has become popular in the United States in the last ten years or so. Its purpose is to avoid giving offence to non-Christians, and it is meant to encompass Thanksgiving, Hanukkah, the New Year and the Winter Solstice. It's becoming increasingly used in the UK, though some dislike it. They argue that it is fatuous to suppose that non-Christians will shudder with indignation at the sound of the word 'Christmas'.

Incidentally, 'Happy Christmas!' as an alternative to 'Merry Christmas' may have its origin in the sensibilities of some Victorian clergymen. 'Merry' suggested 'boozy' and they weren't going to stand for that sort of thing. In fact, 'merry' here comes from the Old English *myrige*, which means 'pleasant' rather than 'jolly'.

According to the Church of England's website, around 3 million people go to a Church of England service on Christmas Eve or Christmas Day.

Between 18th December and Christmas Eve 2011, Sainsbury's distribution centre at Waltham Abbey sent out the following to its shops:

- 100,000 bags of sprouts;
- 15,000 salmon;
- 200,000 bags of clementines;
- enough Coca-Cola to fill two Olympic swimming pools.

In the entire Christmas season, Sainsbury's also sold:

- 5,400,000 mince pies;
- 5,600 tons of cheese;
- enough mulled wine to fill four Olympic swimming pools.

A popular Christmas game at the beginning of the nineteenth century was Hot Cockles. For this festive fun frolic, Player A is blindfolded and places his or her head in the lap of Player B. Other players then take turns to bash player A on the back. Vastly amused by this battering, player A has to identify each assailant. (You may wish to revive the game for your children, as it is cheaper than a Wii or PlayStation.)

Ten Christmas World Records

1. The most expensive Christmas tree was set up in the lobby of the Emirates Palace Hotel in Abu Dhabi in 2010. It was decorated with precious jewellery worth £7 million.
2. The largest group of carol singers (although they were in different places, they were singing at the same time) was in the UK in 2011. 17,117 people took part.
3. The tallest recorded snowman was constructed in Bethel, Maine. It was 122 feet tall. And the scarf was 130 feet long.
4. The smallest snowman is supposed to be the one constructed at the National Physics Laboratory in London in 2009. It was 0.01 mm across (about a fifth of the width of a human hair) and about double that in height. Its eyes and smile were carved on it by an ion beam. However, it is a cheat because it was made of tin and not of snow and thus cannot be considered a *bona fide* snowman. And it didn't have a tiny carrot for a nose, either.
5. The largest Christmas cake was baked in Kerala in India in 2007. It was 30 feet long, 2 feet wide, and weighed 2,500 kgs. It was then cut into 22,000 slices.

(This record can no longer be verified as all the evidence has been eaten.)

6. There is a record for the largest number of people dressed as Father Christmas ice skating while doing the conga. The event took place at Warwick Castle in 2009. 142 Father Christmases took part.

7. Another record is the largest number of scuba divers dressed as Father Christmas. (I am not making this up.) In 2009, the Yorkshire Divers Group achieved this coveted and vital record. 158 divers, dressed as the corpulent crimson conferror, undertook the dive on Christmas Eve 2009. However, it was to raise money for the RNLI, so I shouldn't be so cynical.

8. The oldest surviving letter to Father Christmas dates from 1911. It was written by a brother and sister called Hannah and Fred, who were then ten and seven years old respectively. Hannah requested a doll, a waterproof coat, gloves, a toffee apple, a gold penny, a silver sixpence and a big piece of toffee.

9. Tallest artificial Christmas tree: Mexico City, 2009. Height: 295 feet.

10. Largest number of people dressed as Father Christmas zip-sliding in one hour: 42 people in Rotherham. The zip-slide in question was 70 feet high and 250 feet long. The event raised money for disadvantaged children in South Yorkshire and the North Midlands.

The most watched programme in the UK on Christmas Day 2011 was *EastEnders*, with 9.9 million viewers. Second was *Coronation Street* (9.3 million), third was *Doctor*

Who (8.9 million) and fourth was *Downton Abbey* (8.1 million). Audiences for television programmes are lower in this multi-channel age; in 1986, more than 30 million people watched the Christmas Day episode of *EastEnders* (over half the country's population).

A Christmas Carol

Dickens originally published *A Christmas Carol* on 19th December 1843. It has never been out of print since.

The novella took him six weeks to write. In part, it was based on a story that appeared in *The Pickwick Papers:* an old sexton called Gabriel Grub is converted from his misanthropy by visits from goblins. (The Gabriel Grub story does not show Dickens at his best, it has to be said.) Some have also claimed Dickens was influenced by Jesus' parable of the rich fool (Luke 12.13-21).

Unusually, Dickens paid for the publication out of his own pocket, hoping the profits would be large. In fact, the book cost a great deal to produce – it included hand coloured illustrations and has gilt edged pages – and Dickens earned £744 from it in its first year of publication. By today's prices, that's around £62,000. Most of us would probably be quite pleased with this but Dickens was disappointed. Copies originally cost five shillings – around £20 in today's money. The first print run was 6000 and it had sold out by Christmas Eve.

Stille Nacht (Silent Night) was written in a hurry before the midnight Mass on Christmas Eve 1818. Fr Joseph Mohr was the parish priest of the parish church of St Nicholas in Oberndorf bei Salzburg, Austria. The organ had just broken. Fr Mohr had written the words of the carol a few years before and he dashed over to the organist, Franz Gruber, to see if a tune could be written for guitar accompaniment only.

The carol was one of those sung simultaneously by French, English and German troops during the Christmas truce of 1914. (British officers strongly objected to the idea of Christmas interfering with the serious business of slaughtering people and they issued strict orders for subsequent years that no Christmas truce was to be observed. They further noted that the Christmas truce constituted fraternising with the enemy and was therefore treason.)

A single of *Silent Night,* crooned by Bing Crosby, sold more than ten million copies.

Deeply hilarious Christmas jokes

Christmas Eve at the meat counter. A frantic last minute shopper is anxiously picking over the few remaining turkeys in the hope of finding a large one.

In desperation, he calls over a shop assistant and says, 'Excuse me. Do these turkeys get any bigger?'

'No, mate,' says the shop assistant. 'They're dead.'

What did Adam say on the day before Christmas?
'It's Christmas, Eve.'

A man bought his wife a beautiful diamond ring for Christmas. After hearing about this extravagant gift, a friend of his said, 'I thought she wanted one of those sporty four-wheel-drive vehicles.'

'She did,' he replied. 'Thing is, where was I going to find a fake Jeep?'

Q. If Santa Claus and Mrs Claus had a child, what would he be called?
A. A subordinate claus.

A group of chess grandmasters were seen in a hotel lobby, bragging about their games.

They were, of course, chessnuts boasting in an open foyer.

Essential piece of Christmas correspondence:

Dear Father Christmas,

I can explain...

The Ghost of Christmas Past (Recipes)

Yorkshire Christmas Pie

from Charles Elme Francatelli, The Modern Cook
(London: 1846)

First, bone a turkey, a goose, a brace of young pheasants, four partridges, four woodcocks, a dozen snipes, four grouse, and four widgeons; then boil and trim a small York ham and two tongues. Season and garnish the inside of the fore-named game and poultry, as directed in the foregoing case, with long fillets of fat bacon and tongue, and French truffles; each must be carefully sewn up with a needle and small twine, so as to prevent the force-meat from escaping while they are being baked. When the whole of these are ready, line two round or oval braizing-pans with thin layers of fat bacon, and after the birds have been arranged therein in neat order, and covered in with layers of bacon and buttered paper, put the lids on, and set them in the oven to bake rather slowly, for about four hours: then withdraw them, and allow them to cool.

While the foregoing is in progress, prepare some highly-seasoned aspic-jelly with the carcasses of the game and poultry, to which add six calves'-feet, and the usual complement of vegetables, &c., and when done, let it be clarified: one-half should be reduced previously to its being poured into the pie when it is baked. Make about sixteen pounds of hot-water-paste, and use it to raise a pie of sufficient dimensions to admit of its holding the game and poultry prepared for the purpose, for making which follow the directions contained in the foregoing article. The inside of the pie must first be lined with thin layers of fat bacon, over which spread a coating of well-seasoned force-meat of fat; the birds should then be placed in the following order: – First, put the goose at the bottom with some of the small birds round it, filling up the cavities with some of the force-meat; then, put the turkey and the pheasants with thick slices of the boiled ham between them, reserving the woodcocks and widgeons, that these may be placed on the top: fill the cavities with force-meat and truffles, and cover the whole with thin layers of fat bacon, run a little plain melted butter over the surface, cover the pie in the usual manner, and ornament it with a bold design. The pie must now be baked, for about six hours, in an oven moderately heated, and when taken out, and after the reduced aspic above alluded to has been poured into it, stop the hole up with a small piece of paste, and set it aside in the larder to become cold.

Note. – The quantity of game, &c., recommended to be used in the preparation of the foregoing pie may appear extravagant enough, but it is to be remembered that these very large pies are mostly in request at Christmas time. Their substantial aspect renders them worthy of appearing on the side-table of those wealthy epicures who are wont to keep up the good old English style, at this season of hospitality and good cheer.

Boar's head

From the fourteenth to the fifteenth century, wild boar was often the main dish of a Christmas feast. The head was a particular delicacy

We offer a jovial contemporary song in praise of this product of porcine decapitation, and, in case you want something different for Christmas dinner this year, a recipe for boar's head from 1553.

Here's the song:

> The borys hede that we bryng here
> Betokeneth a Prince withowte pere
> Ys born this day to bye us dere;
> Nowell, nowelle!
>
> This borys hede we bryng with song
> In worchyp of hym that thus sprang
> Of a virgine to redresse all wrong;
> Nowell, nowelle!

And here's the recipe, introduced by its writer:

> In the name of the Holy
> Trinity I, Sabina Welserin,
> begin this cookbook.
> God grant me His holy
> grace and wisdom
> and understanding and judgment
> with which I
> through His Holy will live
> here in this time and
> with Him forever. Amen. anno 1553

To make a boar's head

Take a head, large or small, boil it in water and wine, and when it is done, see to it that the bones remain connected all together, and completely remove the meat from the bones of the head. Pull the rind off carefully, remove the white from the meat and finely chop the remaining boar's head meat, put it in a pan, season it well with pepper, ginger and a little cloves, nutmeg and saffron and let it become good and hot over the fire in the broth in which the head was cooked. Afterwards take the cooked head and place it on a white piece of cloth and lay the skin on the bottom of the cloth, then spread the chopped meat once again on the head and decorate it with the separated skin. And if you do not have enough from one head, then cut the rind from two and decorate the head completely, as if it were whole. After that take the snout and the ears out of the cloth. Also draw the teeth together again with the cloth while it is still hot, so that the head remains intact and let it lie together overnight. In the morning cut the cloth again from the head, then it remains all together. Spread it with a mince of apples, almonds and raisins. Then you have a lordly dish.

from
The good hous-wiues treasurie
Beeing a verye necessarie booke
instructing to the dressing of meates
(1588, anonymous)

To make minst Pyes

Take your Veale and perboyle it a little, or mutton, then set it a cooling; and when it is colde, take three pound of suet to a leg of mutton, or four pound to a fillet of Veale, and then mince them small by themselves, or together whether you will, then take to season them halfe an ounce of Nutmegs, half an ounce of cloves and Mace, halfe an once of Sinamon, a little Pepper, as much Salt as you think will season them, either to the mutton or to the Veale, take viii yolkes of Egges when they be hard, half a pinte of rosewater full measure, halfe an pund of Suger, then straine the Yolkes with the rosewayer and the Suger and mingle it with your meate, if ye have any Orenges or Lemmans you must take two of them, and take the peelles very thin and mince them very smalle, and put them in a pound of currans, six dates, half a pound of prunes laye Currans and Dates upon the top of your meate, you must taek tow or three Pomewaters or Wardens and mince with your meate, if you will make good crust put in three or foure yolkes of egges a litle Rosewater, and a good deale of suger.

The Ghost of Christmas Past (Memories)

from Jane Austen's letters

Steventon: Monday night (December 24). [1798]

My dear Cassandra,

...I returned from Manydown this morning, and found my mother certainly in no respect worse than when I left her. She does not like the cold weather, but that we cannot help. I spent my time very quietly and very pleasantly with Catherine. Miss Blackford is agreeable enough. I do not want people to be very agreeable, as it saves me the trouble of liking them a great deal. I found only Catherine and her when I got to Manydown on Thursday. We dined together and went together to Worting to seek the protection of Mrs Clarke, with whom were Lady Mildmay, her eldest son, and a Mr and Mrs Hoare.

Our ball was very thin, but by no means unpleasant. There were thirty-one people, and only eleven ladies out of the number, and but five single women in the room. Of the gentlemen present you may have some idea from the list of my partners – Mr Wood, G. Lefroy, Rice, a Mr Butcher (belonging to the Temples, a sailor and not of the 11th Light Dragoons), Mr Temple (not the horrid one of all), Mr Wm Orde (cousin to the Kingsclere man), Mr John Harwood, and Mr Calland, who appeared as usual with his hat in his hand, and stood every now and then behind Catherine and me to be talked to and abused for not dancing. We teased him, however, into it at last. I was very glad to see him again after so long a separation, and he was altogether rather the genius and flirt of the evening. He inquired after you.

There were twenty dances, and I danced them all, and without any fatigue. I was glad to find myself capable of dancing so much, and with so much satisfaction as I did; from my slender enjoyment of the Ashford balls (as assemblies for dancing) I had not thought myself equal to it, but in cold weather and with few couples I fancy I could just as well dance for a week together as for half an hour. My black cap was openly admired by Mrs Lefroy, and secretly I imagine by everybody else in the room.

Tuesday. I thank you for your long letter, which I will endeavour to deserve by writing the rest of this as closely as possible. I am full of joy at much of your information; that you should have been to a ball, and have danced at it, and supped with the Prince, and that you should meditate the purchase of a new muslin gown, are delightful circumstances. *I* am determined to buy a handsome one whenever I can, and I am so tired and ashamed of half my present stock, that I even blush at the sight of the wardrobe which contains them. But I will not be much longer libelled by the possession of my coarse spot; I shall turn it into a petticoat very soon. I wish you a merry Christmas, but *no* compliments of the season.

Poor Edward! It is very hard that he, who has everything else in the world that he can wish for, should not have good health too. But I hope with the assistance of stomach complaints, faintnesses, and sicknesses, he will soon be restored to that blessing likewise. If his nervous complaint proceeded from a suppression of something that ought to be thrown out, which does not seem unlikely, the first of these disorders may really be a remedy, and I sincerely wish it may, for I know no one more deserving of happiness without alloy than Edward is.

I cannot determine what to do about my new gown; I wish such things were to be bought ready-made. I have some hopes of meeting Martha at the christening at Deane next Tuesday, and shall see what she can do for me. I want to have something suggested which will give me no trouble of thought or direction.

Again I return to my joy that you danced at Ashford, and that you supped with the Prince. I can perfectly comprehend Mrs Cage's distress and perplexity. She has all those kind of foolish and incomprehensible feelings which would make her fancy herself uncomfortable in such a party. I love her, however, in spite of all her nonsense. Pray give 't'other Miss Austen's' compliments to Edward Bridges when you see him again.

I insist upon your persevering in your intention of buying a new gown; I am sure you must want one, and as you will have 5*l.* due in a week's, time, I am certain you may afford it very well, and if you think you cannot, I will give you the body-lining.

Of my charities to the poor since I came home you shall have a faithful account. I have given a pair of worsted stockings to Mary Hutchins, Dame Kew, Mary Steevens, and Dame Staples; a shift to Hannah Staples, and a shawl to Betty Dawkins; amounting in all to about half a guinea. But I have no reason to suppose that the *Battys* would accept of anything, because I have not made them the offer.

I am glad to hear such a good account of Harriet Bridges; she goes on now as young ladies of seventeen ought to do, admired and admiring, in a much more rational way than her three elder sisters, who had so little of that kind of youth. I dare say she fancies Major Elkington as agreeable as Warren, and if she can think so, it is very well.

... You deserve a longer letter than this; but it is my unhappy fate seldom to treat people so well as they deserve... God bless you!

Yours affectionately,

JANE AUSTEN.

Wednesday. The snow came to nothing yesterday, so I *did* go to Deane, and returned home at nine o'clock at night in the little carriage, and without being very cold.

from The Parish Magazine of Linton, Cambridgeshire. A description by the Reverend John Longe of the meal given to the poor of the village.

On Christmas Day over a hundred of the aged poor were supplied at the soup kitchen with an ample dinner of hot boiled beef, dumplings and vegetables, which they took to their houses, and there, no doubt, enjoyed most thoroughly. They also received a gift of tea and sugar, and in the case of any old man being a smoker, some tobacco. This is the second year they have been so regaled through the kindness of Mr and Mrs Gotliebb Brinkmann, whom we all hope soon to welcome to the Parish. Our best thanks are due to Mr And Mrs Nichols and Miss Jessie Currie for their care and trouble in arranging for and dispensing the dinners so successfully.

from The Journal of Sir Walter Scott

1826

December 31. It must be allowed that the regular recurrence of annual festivals among the same individuals has, as life advances, something in it that is melancholy. We meet on such occasions like the survivors of some perilous expedition, wounded and weakened ourselves, and looking through the diminished ranks of those who remain, while we think of those who are no more. Or they are like the feasts of the Caribs, in which they held that the pale and speechless phantoms of the deceased appeared and mingled with the living. Yet where shall we fly from vain repining? Or why should we give up the comfort of seeing our friends, because they can no longer be to us, or we to them, what we once were to each other?

1827

December 21. A very sweet pretty-looking young lady, the Prima Donna of the Italian Opera, now performing here, by name Miss Ayton, came to breakfast this morning, with her father, (a bore, after the manner of all fathers, mothers, aunts, and other chaperons of pretty actresses)! Miss Ayton talks very prettily, and, I dare say, sings beautifully, though too much in the Italian manner, I fear, to be a great favourite of mine. But I did not hear her, being called away by the Clerk's coach. I am like Jeremy in *Love for Love* – have a reasonable good ear for a jig, but your solos and sonatas give me the spleen.

December 23. Went to church to Borthwick with the family, and heard a well-composed, well-delivered, sensible discourse from Mr Wright, the clergyman – a different sort of person, I wot, from my old half-mad, half-drunken, little hump-back acquaintance [the Reverend John] Clunie, renowned for singing 'The Auld Man's Mear's dead,' and from the circumstance of his being once interrupted in his minstrelsy by the information that his own horse had died in the stable.

Samuel Taylor Coleridge
Ratzeburg, Germany, 1799

There is a Christmas custom here which pleased and interested me. The children make little presents to their parents, and to each other; and the parents to the children. For three or four months before Christmas the girls are all busy, and the boys save up their pocket-money, to make or purchase these presents. What the present is to be is cautiously kept secret, and the girls have a world of contrivances to conceal it – such as working when they are out on visits, and the others are not with them; getting up in the morning before day-light, and the like. Then, on the evening before Christmas Day, one of the parlours is lighted up by the children, into which the parents must not go. A great yew bough is fastened on the table at a little distance from the wall, a multitude of tapers are fastened in the bough, but so as not to catch it till they are nearly burnt out, and coloured paper hangs and flutters from the twigs. Under this bough the children lay out in great order the presents they mean for their parents, still concealing in their pockets what they intend for each other. Then the parents are introduced, and each presents his little gift, and then bring out the rest one by one from their pockets, and present them with kisses and embraces. When I witnessed this scene there were eight or nine children, and the eldest daughter and the mother wept aloud for joy and tenderness; and the tears ran down the face of the father, and he clasped all his children so tight to his breast, it seemed as if he did it to stifle the sob that was rising within him. I was very much affected.'

We consider Christmas as the encounter, the great encounter, the historical encounter, the decisive encounter, between God and mankind. He who has faith knows this truly; let him rejoice.

Pope Paul VI

When we were children we were grateful to those who filled our stockings at Christmas time. Why are we not grateful to God for filling our stockings with legs?

G.K. Chesterton

The Church does not superstitiously observe days, merely as days, but as memorials of important facts. Christmas might be kept as well upon one day of the year as another; but there should be a stated day for commemorating the birth of our Saviour, because there is danger that what may be done on any day, will be neglected.

Samuel Johnson

People can't concentrate properly on blowing other people to pieces if their minds are poisoned by thoughts suitable to the twenty-fifth of December.

Ogden Nash

Mankind is a great, an immense family. This is proved by what we feel in our hearts at Christmas.

Pope John XXIII